Rogue Black

SPECIAL RESERVE. DO NOT
DISCARD OR ISSUE FREELY.

Raymond Giles

CORONET BOOKS
Hodder Fawcett Ltd., London

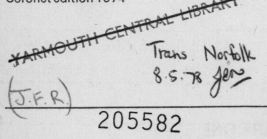

~~YARMOUTH CENTRAL LIBRARY~~

Trans Norfolk
8·5·78 Jen

(J.F.R)

205582

*The characters and situations in this book are
entirely imaginary and bear no relation to any real
person or actual happening.*

Printed and bound in Great Britain for
Coronet Books, Hodder Fawcett Ltd,
St. Paul's House, Warwick Lane,
London, EC4P 4AH
By C. Nicholls & Company Ltd,
The Philips Park Press, Manchester

ISBN 0 340 18610 0

PART ONE

chapter one

He had been warned.

"Remember, boy, you're black—she's white! She's free, you're a slave! You and me, beside her we're nothing! But her—next time I see you touch her, I'll make you bleed! I spent too much time educating you to see you die!"

Simon, the majordomo—tall as an angel, black as death, handsome as a cat—had warned him time and again. "You and that girl, you're not babies any longer, boy, and you can't *be* together like babies! You're turning into a man, and she's turning into a woman—and don't you know that a white woman is death for a black man?" *But not for you, Simon, not for you.* "Don't you know what happens to the nigger that touches a white woman?" *But not to you, Simon.* "The whipping is like none you've ever seen. They use a rawhide whip that takes off your skin, then they grind salt into your flesh till you think you're dying in fire. But that's only the beginning, boy, because before they're done with you, you're not a man anymore. That's right, they take that away from you, and they make sure you know they're taking it, and you're never going to get it back again. And then, if you're lucky, maybe they kill you—but they do it slowly, a little bit at a time!"

He had been warned.

But what did the warnings mean? What did they have to do, really, with him? Or with Hannah?

She was his earliest memory. He had been named Tracy after her mother, and he and Hannah had virtually been raised together. The relationship was a common one between black and white children: he, some eighteen months the older, was her playmate and protector, a surrogate older brother. He had learned early that he was black; only much later did it occur to him that she was white.

He had frequently been bathed in the same tub with her, had often slept in the same bed. She had worn the same thin, cotton, knee-length shirts that he and all other plantation infants had worn, when they wore anything at all; and during the oven-hot days of summer, she had played naked in the dust with the other children, her body turning to a rich copper-brown, only a shade or two lighter than his. When the chill rains came at the end of summer, he had often been admitted to the great white mansion, almost as if it were his own home—he and Hannah had eaten together in the pantry. And the two of them had often huddled together in their cotton shirts before Simon's fireplace, listening to his stories of Golden Apples and Minotaurs, until they fell asleep at last and dreamed away the night in the majordomo's cottage.

They had grown up together. The relationship had continued even after Hannah's mother had died and her widowed aunt had come to the plantation to look after her. . . . And everybody knew (quietly, secretly, the truth only whispered) about Simon and Aunt Rachel.

So why should the warnings have meant anything to Tracy?

"You're black—she's white! Next time I see you touch her, I'll make you bleed!"

But how could he help but touch her? They belonged to each other, in a way, and she was even bolder and more curious than he.

Yet, in time, they did drift apart. He was trusted to help in the stables, and Simon taught him to be a houseboy. He still saw Hannah almost daily, but he became a half-hand, a three-quarter-hand, and finally a prime full-hand, and his days were full and busy. Besides, the time came when the eighteen months between them made a difference, in his view, and she was still too much a child while he had become completely a man. There were other girls, now.

Then one day in his seventeenth summer he rediscovered Hannah, and she him, and the eighteen months between them vanished.

Six days of the week were devoted to cultivating the cane fields and cutting wood for the sugarhouse and preparing the barrels and hogsheads. The Carter slaves were well treated and cared for, as slave life went, but still they sweated for their hog-fat and grits under a hard sun and the fire of the lash. Relief came on Saturday evening. Then the hands returned early from the fields, each free to do as he pleased as long as he didn't interfere with the pleasure of another. Supper was long and leisurely and, for some, continued for the rest of the night. Some made the music that came from the slave quarter, others preferred to dance to it. Those who had partners, or could find them, made love. Jugs were broken out, jugs that the master and the overseer pretended not to know of as long as the liquor poisoned no one. Even fights were permitted, as long as they were between two willing and unarmed men or women.

Sunday morning was quiet time. Those who enjoyed prayer meetings were allowed to have them, those who wished to sleep late could do so, those who wished to cultivate their own garden patches seized the opportunity.

In the afternoon, if the weather was good, many went swimming. That was where Tracy rediscovered Hannah and forgot all the warnings.

As the sun grew hotter, the slaves gathered at one of the few good places for swimming on the plantation, a stretch of gravel-bottomed stream where the water ran clear. By early afternoon, perhaps fifty blacks played in the sparkling water, while dozens more sat in the shade along the banks, and still the crowd grew. Men, wearing pants torn short and beyond repair, waded through the water, splashing and shouting like children. Women bobbed down into

the water to come up with old cotton dresses and torn
shifts clinging wetly to their bodies, then shrieked as men
pursued them. Couples wandered off alone from time to
time, returned, and sometimes wandered off again. Children, a few white but most of them black, played naked in
the shallows, yelling, weeping, chattering.

Tracy, walking along the bank, saw Hannah.

It was the first time she had appeared for the swimming
this summer, and she had appeared only a time or two the
summer before. He hadn't thought about her absence,
hadn't expected to see her; after all, she had turned sixteen only a week ago, and he had worked at the party her
Aunt Rachel had given in her honor. At sixteen, most
well-to-do young white ladies from these parts had some
idea of who their future husbands would be, and Hannah
was no exception: everybody knew she would marry
Ethan Flynn. Many people would have said she was now
too old to be out playing with the blacks on a lazy Sunday
afternoon, yet here she was.

She wore the same knee-length white cotton shift so
commonly worn by women, black and white, as a working
garment; Tracy had seldom seen her wearing anything
else. Her hair fell loose to her shoulders and swirled about
her face like a jet-black cloud. Her arms were barely
tanned this year, and her calves were white, but the color
of her face was high. She waded near the edge of the
stream, looking after a group of small children, patting
and herding them, lifting and carrying them, laughing with
them. Tracy watched for a moment, and he understood:
Hannah was showing that she was grown up now, old
enough to mother children; but at the same time, she was
here because she wanted nothing to change, she wanted to
cling to her own childhood.

She saw him, and she smiled. Then the smile, through
self-consciousness, became a crooked grin, and she stuck
her tongue out at him.

"What's the matter," she called to him, "skirred of the
water?"

He felt an odd embarrassment, as if everyone were suddenly staring at him, and he could only think to say,
"What do *you* know!" as he hurriedly stepped off the

bank. The water felt shockingly cold, and the gravel was unkind to his feet.

"Skirred of the water!" she said as he waded toward her.

"I don't see you getting wet."

She backed away from him, going into deeper water, and he followed. The water was like ice coming up on his thighs, but it didn't seem to bother Hannah a bit. She splashed water at him, and he gasped as it hit his bare belly.

"Skirred, skirred, skirred!" she chanted, grinning at him and continuing to splash. "Skirred to get yo' pecker wet, skirred to get yo' pecker wet, skirred, skirred, skirred!"

He lunged at her, thinking to grab and duck her, but she twisted and darted away. He saw a flash of white buttocks through wet white cotton, and then he was plunging down through the chilling water. He flailed about until he regained his footing, and he came up choking and coughing. By the time he had cleared his eyes of water, Hannah was thirty feet away.

He went after her, weaving through the crowd that played in the stream. She stood knee-deep in water, looking as if in the last half-minute she had completely forgotten his existence. When she saw him, her eyes widened, and she screamed, but by then it was too late. While the crowd around them laughed, he toppled her off of her feet and dragged her into deeper water, shoving her beneath the surface. He stepped back and waited.

She staggered to her feet, snorting and moaning, head down, her hair about her face. She pulled her shift away from the front of her body and shook herself, almost like a dog. When she cleared her face of hair, he saw that she was frowning, and she spoke in an angry voice, too low for anyone but him to hear.

"You bastard!"

"What'd I do?" he asked, shocked.

"You got my hair all wet, you bastard. I didn't want to get my hair all wet!"

"Skirred to get yo' hair wet," he mocked, "skirred to get yo' hair wet. Skirred, skirred, skirred—"

She giggled and tripped him before he realized what

was happening. It was neatly done: he fell on his back in the deeper water, floundered, and sank, kicking and strangling. For one panicky, moment, he thought he might actually be drowning, and it seemed to take forever for him to fight his way back up out of the water. When at last he could look about again, she had disappeared from sight.

He waded downstream a few yards, but she was nowhere in the water or along the bank; by the time he turned upstream again, he was becoming angry with her: she had no right to leave him like this. Then, turning a bend in the stream, he saw her standing in the water some fifty feet away, and his anger instantly vanished. Again, he went after her.

She saw him, laughed at him, and fled in a glistening spray of water. The water rose on her legs and fell again as she ran, paddled, fell splashing, and climbed to her feet to run again, scrambling between the other waders and swimmers. And Tracy pursued, hardly realizing they were playing the same ancient game he had often watched others play, knowing only that he had to reach her.

She ran with amazing speed; he closed the distance between them with more difficulty than he would have expected. Then suddenly the others were left behind, and the banks of the stream were bare of people. The sun burned down like white-hot iron. The stream meandered more here, and the knee-deep water flowed slow and warm. Hannah disappeared around a bend, and as Tracy followed her, he grew alarmed. The gravel had given way to the alluvial silt more common in this part of the country, and as it squeezed unpleasantly between his toes, he thought of water moccasins and copperheads. Then he thought of quicksands and bottomless mud pits into which a person might sink. . . . He had to reach Hannah and keep her from running farther.

The bank was steep at that point, and he climbed it with difficulty, only to find that Hannah was now much farther away from him. Yet they hardly ran, but merely walked or trotted along the stream, as if they both knew what would inevitably happen.

They passed no other swimmers, saw no one. The sun dried them at once, and they began to burn. Then, at last,

Tracy saw where Hannah was leading him: there was another stretch of gravel-bottom stream ahead, the water comparatively clear, with a familiar patch of woods on the other side. He remembered having been here with Hannah years before. Pleased, he ran to catch up with her, as she ran ahead, splashing her way into the stream.

He followed, and again the water seemed icy-cold for a minute on his over-heated skin. He thrashed after Hannah, caught her by the arms, and they fell laughing. She tore loose from him and splashed him, and he splashed back. They grappled. A kind of longing flooded over Tracy.

They both plunged deeply into the water, almost to the bed of the stream, clinging together, and the longing grew.

They came up in water that was hip-deep on him and almost to her waist. They faced each other, her forehead on his shoulder, each holding the other's arms and steadying themselves. He blinked the water from his eyes. Hannah's wet shift clung to her, and it was as if he were looking at her naked body through a film of milk. He shivered as if the day had suddenly turned cold, though the sun continued to burn and not a breeze stirred the air.

"You're beautiful," he said.

He hadn't meant to say it; he hadn't meant to speak at all.

She lifted her head and looked at him. Her eyes were deeply, impossibly blue, almost a purple; he had never before known that eyes could be such a color. He was sure he had never really looked at Hannah's before.

A wisp of a smile played at the corners of her mouth, as if she wanted to smile but was a little afraid.

"You still like me?" she asked.

"Like you? Course I like you, I always liked you."

"I thought you stopped."

"No, I never stopped. You were just sort of a baby for a while longer'n me."

She looked down at her own body: breasts and belly. "Ain't no baby now," she said meditatively. "Take a look."

13

Tracy shivered again. "Don't talk like that. It ain't fitten."

Hannah wrinkled her nose and briefly stuck out her tongue. "You like me as much as Simon likes Aunt Rachel?" she asked.

The question shocked Tracy. Though it was spoken without innuendo, its effect was to say openly what was never said openly—that there was something special about the relationship between the black majordomo and the white woman. Tracy understood that Hannah was also asking if he liked her the way Simon liked her Aunt Rachel.

He didn't have to answer. The tug of desire, suddenly unleashed, answered for him. Hannah laughed, stepped back, and sprayed water on him; he splashed back as much as he could, and again they were romping in the stream like children. He seized her wrists, tripped her up, and threw her down in the water, trying not to think of how much he wanted her.

But then they were on their knees in the water, wrestling together, and—clumsily, childishly—she kissed him.

She's going to marry Ethan Flynn, he thought. Not *She's white and I'm black,* not *She's free and I'm a slave,* but *She's going to marry Ethan Flynn.*

And I love her.

"Do you *really* like me?" she asked.

"I love you." He could do no more than whisper.

"Then I guess it's all right if I kiss you, ain't it? Anything that's all right for Aunt Rachel and Simon is all right for you and me, ain't it?"

"You gon' marry Ethan."

"Oh, I don't know." She tossed her head. "I just may, or I just may not. Ain't made up my mind yet."

"You shouldn't say *ain't,*" he said inanely. "Your daddy and your aunt don't like it. Neither do—neither does Simon."

"My daddy don't give a damn, and neither do I. I do as I please, and right now I feel like swimming skinny. Let's take our clothes off."

Again, he felt a pang of shock, one that almost chilled his desire for her.

"We shouldn't," he said breathlessly.

"Why not? We done it lots of times before." She was already lifting her shift, but she paused and stared at him.

"That was different," he said. "We older now."

"We *are* older," she corrected him mockingly, "only we're not so much. Anyway, what's the difference? Lots of older people swim skinny, too, you know. Didn't you ever go swimming nekkid with a growed-up girl before?"

"Lots of times," he lied.

She stood up and began pulling her shift the rest of the way off. "Then what are you skirred of?" she asked. "Just 'cause you got yo' pecker up? Honestly, Tracy, sometimes you are so dumb."

Her barnyard frankness was a kind of innocence, and it banished his inhibitions. As she pulled her shift over her head and tossed it onto a bank of the stream, he stood up, kicked away his pants, and tossed them after her shift. She splashed him and ran away.

They circled and splashed, circled and splashed, ran up into the shallow water, dived back into the deep. They grappled a few times, sometimes kissed hastily, even more hastily broke apart. She teased him about his desire, but it was more than desire he felt, and he had difficulty in teasing her in return. She slapped, pinched, grabbed at him and ran away, and he pursued her up onto a bank, caught her and rolled her in the grass, and let her escape back into the pool again.

He wanted her. He felt as if this could end in only one way, and yet at the same time, he felt that it never would. He hardly cared. The important thing was that he loved her and she wanted to be here with him.

He caught her again in thigh-deep water, and they wrestled hand-to-shoulder, head-to-head, bodies apart. The hot sunlight reflected by the water was blinding, and their skin seemed to sizzle as the heat bit into it. His lips went to her ear.

"I told you I love you," he said.

"I know that."

"Tell me that you love me. Just once. Even if you don't mean it."

"I love you."

"But you don't mean it?"

"I *do* mean it, you dumb Tracy, I *do* love you, I *do!*"

His mouth found hers more expertly now, and her hands slid over his body without leaving it. They held each other, and he saw her eyes glaze and begin to close.

Then her eyes widened again, and she broke away from him with a wail of terror and despair.

Ethan Flynn was undoubtedly one of the most envied youths in Louisiana. At nineteen, he was well over six feet tall, and this in a time and place when most men were five feet ten or less. He had a round, placid, good-natured face and a lazy grin, which both men and women found attractive. He was heavily and strongly built, but he moved with a lightness and grace that made him appear slimmer and more catlike than he was.

He had many acquaintances. If his real friends were few, this was partly because he was envied, partly because his lazy grin could become a sneer, and partly because he had so little conception of what friendship was. Still, he was usually surrounded by young men who acknowledged his leadership, and from the time he entered his teens, he never failed to find available women. There were the slaves, of course, both the willing and the unwilling: it was said that he enjoyed every female on the Flynn plantations who reached adolescence with a certain amount of attractiveness. And then there were the poor-white women, the tenant wives and their daughters, who gave themselves to him either from fear or in hope of favors. But such wretches were by no means the only women Ethan Flynn was acquainted with. More than one wealthy plantation wife blushed at certain memories, even while her daughter was preparing blushes of her own.

Some of Ethan's oat-sowing was known, but it was glossed over as being just that: a young man's inconsequential escapades before settling down. It was rumored that Ethan had stabbed to death a white farmer who had caught him with his daughter, but this was never proved. Nor were certain accusations that Ethan had raped this or that slave girl or cut up this or that black man. He was a knife fighter, no doubt, and a good one, but this was simply one more cause for envy. The important thing was that he had spirit—and that he had cut up none of the wrong people and left no bastards in the wrong places.

He was an only son, and heir to three great plantations and a number of tenant farms. His future was assured. He was rich, and he would be richer when he married Hannah Carter.

He had, ever since he could remember, simply assumed that he would do this. The principal Carter and Flynn plantations were right next to each other, the two mansions only minutes apart, and the families had been friends for generations; now at last, they would become one and the same. Hannah Carter had no brothers, and her name would become Flynn.

Hannah Carter was heir to four of the greatest cane and cotton plantations in the Delta states, plus an unknown number of tenant farms. Ethan figured that after he had married her, he would be one of the richest planters—perhaps the very richest—in the entire South.

He had dreams, never divulged, about how he would live. Women would be his for the taking, of course, women who had refused him in the past and women he had yet to meet. He would spend much of his time in the cities—New Orleans, Memphis, St. Louis. He had a taste for gambling and a taste for blood wagers—cockfights, dogfights, knife fights. He would live like a pagan king.

Hannah? She would be no problem. A king needed a queen, and he was astonished to see how beautiful she was becoming. He felt that he deserved her and that she was worthy of him. He was not at all surprised that she apparently shared the common assumption that they would marry. She was the key to his future as he envisioned it, and nothing could be allowed to go wrong. Though her beauty took his breath away, and though he had had girls far younger than she, he would never under any circumstances have touched her until the right time came. It was coming; he could wait.

Besides, in some mysterious way Hannah was different from the others. It never occurred to Ethan that he could marry some woman other than Hannah—he had no respect for any other. Nor did it occur to him that the very fact that he planned to marry Hannah was what made her different. He was going to marry her; therefore it was impossible to believe that she was as corrupt, as fallible, as animal, as *real* as the other women he had known.

But of course he put up with the usual joking from his male companions, taking it as a compliment.

"You been gettin' any of that stuff, Ethan?"

"Sure, Ethan's been gettin' it. Everybody knows that little gal's his."

"Yeah, but is he gettin *enough* of it? And on the other hand, is he givin' that little gal enough to keep *her* happy?"

"Why? Do you intend to help Ethan out?"

"Sure, if he'll let me. Seems like that's the least one friend can do for another. How 'bout it, Ethan? You want me to help you boost that little gal?"

"Don't mind him, Ethan, He's got so little boost in him that all he can do is think about it and talk."

They were joking with him about Hannah on the Sunday afternoon that everything changed.

They had vague plans of having a swim, finding some women, doing some drinking. Six of them, Ethan and five others, wandered through the Flynn and Carter fields, looking for a usable bathing spot that hadn't already been preempted by the blacks. Ethan had in mind one he had sometimes visited on the Carter plantation.

"Yeah, that Hannah is really growing up to be something! If Ethan don't bed her down soon, one of us has got to do something about it!"

"Oh, man you so far behind the times, you ain't funny. Don't you know Ethan been taking care of her since she was eleven years old?"

"That right? Eleven years old, Ethan?"

"Ten. You all be quiet. I think there's somebody in our swimming hole."

They all came to a halt and glanced at each other. Then, following Ethan's lead, they moved silently forward through the woods toward the stream. Ethan had seen nothing—the trees and brush blocked the view—but he was certain he had heard a laugh. A woman's laugh.

He continued until he had a clear view of the stream

and the two people. At first, Ethan saw only that they were a black man and a white girl, standing naked in the water and whispering like lovers. Their mouths met, and their hands moved over each other's body.

Then he saw that the black man was Tracy, a Carter houseboy, and the white girl was Hannah Carter.

His Hannah.

No one would have guessed from his appearance what was happening within him. No one would have guessed what was happening to his conception of himself and Hannah, of his future and the world he lived in.

His Hannah!

"Boys," he said quietly, calmly, "I think I'm just gon' cut me a little nigger meat."

Tracy had been warned. But he had never dreamed it would be anything like this.

There were a half-dozen of them around him in the stream. He recognized most of them: Ethan Flynn, a couple of the Colby boys, one of the Folletts. Every one of them was holding up a knife—every one but Ethan, who stood back from the others and grinned, and his grin seemed even more dangerous, more threatening, than the knives.

They moved slowly around him. He realized he could no longer hear Hannah crying out, and he had no idea of where she might be. He had never before felt more naked or more vulnerable.

"Hey, son," one of the Colbys said, "would you look at that boy's eyes roll."

"Just like hard-boiled eggs."

"They ain't the only eggs gon' roll."

They all laughed, and Ethan's grin broadened. Tracy tried to back away from them, but they were always behind him, always moving around him, always holding up the long flashing blades.

"Move him up onto the bank," Ethan said casually, almost as if bored. "You've got him where he can climb up easy now."

"You hear, boy?" said a nameless blond youth. "You climb up on that bank."

Tracy at last found his voice, but it hardly sounded like his own. "What you gon' do?"

"What we gon' do! I think you know what we gon' do, boy."

That's right, they take that away from you, and they make sure you know they're taking it, and you're never going to get it back again. And then, if you're lucky, maybe they kill you—but they do it slowly, a little bit at a time!

The circle around Tracy opened to allow him to climb up on the bank, but now he didn't want to move. His hands involuntarily closed over his genitals, and he found his knees bending and his back hunching.

"Now, ain't that cute."

"He gettin' sorta modest, ain't he."

"He better while he got a chance. He ain't gon' have nothing to be modest about pretty soon."

A sob escaped from Tracy in spite of himself. He knew that these grinning white boys were serious. He had been caught with a white girl—worse, with a white girl marked for Ethan. He was *not* Simon, and she was *not* her Aunt Rachel, and these whites meant to castrate him and, in all likelihood, eventually kill him. Now all the warnings he had received from Simon took on meaning. He remembered all the stories he had heard about slaves who had been burned alive, tortured, hung. But he had never thought that such a thing could happen to him. Not to him.

Ethan and a redheaded boy were climbing up on the bank a few yards away. Tracy remained where he was, half circled by the other four.

"Get up that bank!" Follett commanded.

"No."

"Nigger, we can cut you up just as good here in the water," one of the Colbys said, "but I don't want to foul up the stream with nigger shit. Now, get up that bank!"

"No."

"Get up—"

Colby jabbed the tip of his knife into Tracy's hip. Tracy screamed, less from pain than from rage and terror, and without thinking, he swung his arm backhanded as hard as he could. He caught Colby on the side of the head, knocking him backwards into the water. All of them, even Colby, laughed.

At that moment, Tracy saw one wild hope. Ethan and the redhead were on their knees on the bank. One of the Colbys was sitting down in the water. All six whites were momentarily distracted with laughter, and he was no longer surrounded.

He scrambled up the bank like a monkey. His feet kept slipping, and the climb seemed to take forever, and he expected to feel a hand or a knife blade at any instant. But then he was up on the bank, and he was running, and there was no one ahead of him. He was free.

He heard cheers and laughter behind him, and he knew they wanted him to run: this was part of their sport, part of the agony they were putting him through. But he had no choice; he could only try to run faster, run blindly, run through the woods like a terrified animal. He heard wails coming from his throat; he couldn't stop them. Tough though his feet were, running this hard was torture: sticks and stones cut into his feet like metal and glass. But worse was the knowledge that knives and torture and perhaps even death were pursuing him.

He slipped and fell to one knee. He got up immediately and threw himself forward, still running with all his strength. He slipped again and fell full-length. When he climbed to his feet, he found that his right knee had been badly twisted, and he could barely hobble.

The Follett boy appeared in front of him, grinning, panting, knife in hand.

Tracy turned to the right and almost ran into the Colby boy he had knocked down. He looked to the left and saw the other Colby and the redhead.

"Want to run some more, nigger?" the redhead asked, and Tracy realized that the six were again circling around him. Or rather five were circling him, while Ethan stood to one side, smiling lazily and sucking on a blade of grass.

"He don't want to run," said the blond boy. "He plumb tuckered out."

"He stop runnin'," Follett said. "Ain't nothing to do but bob his tail."

"Look at them eyes roll!"

"They gon' roll a lot more when I slice him open and hand him his guts."

"He gon' wish we finish him off."

"Oh, he got a long time to live yet. He just ain't gon' enjoy it none."

The knives flashed.

"Move, nigger!"

"Move!"

He moved, he didn't know how. His right knee was stiffening fast, and he had to grab at trees and at brush to help himself along. He thought he was weeping, but he couldn't be sure. When he paused or hesitated, a knife would come at him, sometimes merely passing dangerously close, sometimes leaving a long thin line of blood or a deeper jab. His body stung as if he had been attacked by hornets. He wanted to refuse to move any farther; he would have preferred to stand still and die with some dignity. But he knew he could not. Somehow they would see that dignity was denied him.

"All right," Ethan said, "that's enough. Put him on his back."

He knew what came next, and he fought them. He struck out at them, he bit, he clawed, he tried to grab their knives.

"By God, he's a strong nigger!"

"Strong for a house nigger."

"That what he is? He ain't gon' be strong before long."

"On his back, I said! Damn it, get him down!"

"Here he goes!"

Tracy strained every muscle, even those in his pain-racked leg. Five men were on him, while Ethan stood by smiling, and it took all five to hold him down. His naked body was slick with sweat and blood, and he didn't let his captors relax for a moment.

"Now, get his knees up to his shoulders. Keep his legs wide apart."

"Ethan, he won't stay still—"

"Do as I tell you, damn it. Once you've got his knees to his shoulders, he'll hardly be able to move. And he'll be able to see what we're doing to him.

. . . they make sure you know they're taking it, and you're never going to get it back again. . . .

He still fought them, but he couldn't stop them.

"That's right, get his butt up in the air." Ethan sounded as calm as ever. "Boy, do you know who I am?"

Tracy couldn't answer.

"Well, I know who you are, you're that Carter house nigger—Stacey, Lacy, something like that. You listen to me, Stacey. I want you to see what I'm doing to you." As he spoke, Ethan took out a knife for the first time. It came from a sheath inside the front of his trousers, and it was not a very big knife—about five thin inches of carbon steel. "Now, don't you go closing your eyes, Stacey, 'cause if you do, one of these boys is likely to stick a little old point in your eyes, and then you ain't never going to see *any*thing again. You understand?"

"He understand all right," said one of the Colbys, who was straining to hold Tracy's right leg.

Ethan knelt. Tracy felt as if he were already dying when Ethan reached for him, and hot acid rose in his throat and spilled from his mouth.

"Better hurry," Follett said. "I think this nigger gon' pass out."

"I don't hardly knew where to begin," Ethan said, tightening his fingers and bringing the steel edge to the flesh.

The steel moved, and then it stopped. Tracy saw huge black hands closing on Ethan's wrists, and the white hands were lifted away. Ethan himself was lifted away and flung aside. He saw Simon, and Simon was speaking, but all the words signified to Tracy was one long roar of anger.

The other five whites leaped away from Tracy as if on command. Voices were raised, and knives were still out, but Simon held the others at bay by the very strength of his rage. Looking up, Tracy saw him as a great black giant, far taller than Ethan or any of the others, threatening at any moment to hurl a thunderbolt.

Gradually words took on meaning again. "How dare you put a knife to one of Mr. Carter's slaves without ever a word to him! What the hell are you, a bunch of goddam Georgia rednecks? Christ, Mr. Ethan, I thought you of all people had more sense—"

"Don't you talk to me about sense, Simon—"

"You're on Carter property, and you're abusing Carter property, and I am speaking for Mr. Carter, and you had better believe it!"

"If you know what the nigger done—"

"I'd say what I'm saying now! Go tell Mr. Carter!"

"I will!"

Tracy had never heard a black man speak to a white man as Simon had just spoken to Ethan Flynn and his friends. But he didn't think about that now. All he thought about now was that he wasn't going to be mutilated and killed after all.

chapter two

Addison Carter sat in his favorite chair at the end of the long drawing room. The chair looked somewhat like a throne and he, when he sat on it, like a monarch; the fact amused him, when he thought about it. He was quite aware that he possessed more wealth and power than many a feudal lord. There were laws, of course, but when one had wealth and power, they could usually be bent where white men were concerned and brushed aside in the case of blacks. Addison Carter held the power of life and death.

At the moment, he was faintly bored. Boredom was his reaction to disgust, and disgust his reaction to violence. He regarded himself as a civilized man.

"I admit I was wrong in taking a knife to that nigger without coming to you first," Ethan said, "but, my God, any decent white man would have done the same. Wouldn't you have done the same, sir?"

Addison ignored the question and looked at the boy with some faint interest. Ethan was on his best behavior now, trying to speak grammatically and full of a white man's self-righteousness. He was trying to be what he supposed other people expected him to be. Addison didn't particularly like the boy, but then he didn't particularly like any of the young men of the region. If Hannah had to marry—and young women *were* inclined to do so—he supposed Ethan would do as well as any boy and no doubt better than some.

"I said, sir, wouldn't you have done—"

"I heard you." Addison seldom raised his voice. "The question is irrelevant and impertinent. Have you anything more to say?"

"Yes, sir. I suppose I should thank that big buck nigger of yours for stopping me till I got my temper back—"

"Indeed you should," Addison murmured.

"But now let's do the job right."

"Do the job right?"

"Castrate the nigger and string him up. Or, better yet, burn him—"

"Castrate him, kill him? But why?"

"Why, make him an example," Ethan said, as if the fact were obvious. "We can't let a nigger get away with anything like this!"

"Get away with what?" Addison plucked at his lower lip and purposely looked somewhat bewildered.

Ethan's face reddened. "Sir, I saw them myself! I told you—don't you believe me? They were both of them jay-bird naked—"

"I'm not terribly surprised. They were raised together, you know, and sometimes they still act like pickaninnies—"

"They weren't acting like pickaninnies, Mr. Carter—"

"Sir, are you telling me that you have no interest in marrying my daughter?"

The question was posed quietly and with a shrug of the shoulders, and Addison was pleased to see that it brought Ethan up short. The boy stood there with his mouth hanging open and his eyes blank.

"No—no," he stammered after a moment, "I didn't mean that—"

"Good. I *was* under the impression that you had some such interest. Since you retain that interest, I'm sure that

26

there's not the faintest doubt in your mind that she is a fine upright young woman, virtuous, God-fearing, and beyond any hint of a doubt a virgin."

"Well . . . of course . . ."

"Then what in the world is all this fuss about?"

For a moment Addison thought Ethan was going to lose control of himself. "Goddammit, sir," he roared, "you didn't *see* them!"

It was time to work toward a compromise. "You're quite right. I didn't see them. And furthermore, they're both too old to continue the privileges accorded to children. What starts innocently—and I have no doubt that what has happened today did start innocently—could very well have tragic consequences. I think we're agreed on that?"

"Well . . . yes, sir." Ethan sounded uncertain.

"Good. Fortunately, you arrived in time to see that there was not the slightest question of such consequences, but we must be certain that no such incident occurs again. I shall see to that. *Your* job is to see to your friends."

"Sir?"

"You had five lads with you. Now, we can hardly prevent them from spreading tales about what they saw, but I trust that you can keep them from telling tales about what they did *not* see. You're quite right in being worried about this matter," a little sugar, Addison thought, "since people are apt to let their imaginations run riot when given the chance. Do you follow me?"

"I think so."

"The more I think about it, the more I can understand why you were so hard on poor Tracy. He really should have known better, even if Hannah didn't. After all, the only thing your friends actually saw was a boy and a girl —who had been raised together—wading in a stream. But once their fertile imaginations get to working, who knows what they'll say about your future wife? Unless you can stop them. Can you?"

"I guess I can. If you can do something about that nigger."

"Of course. But no more nonsense about castration and

hanging." Addison smiled grimly. "I'd rather the boy lived to rue the day. And now I suggest you rejoin your friends."

Ethan left the room, and Addison breathed a sigh of relief. He was reasonably certain now that he had the situation under control, though a good deal of unpleasantness still lay ahead. He just hoped to God that Hannah had had the sense not to lie to him when he had talked to her in her room.

"No, Daddy, he didn't do a thing to me! Honest, I tell you, honest, he didn't! All we did was go wading and swimming and splashing 'round like we always done!"

She had come running toward the house, naked, screaming like a child. Only she wasn't a child anymore. But, to him, she did seem to be one, when she had put on a fresh white shift.

"Hannah, I'm asking you one more time. Shall I send for the doctor? Don't be afraid to tell me. If you think there might be the slightest reason—"

"But what for? 'Cause you still think I might get me a pickaninny?"

"Hannah, I don't even know if you know how—"

"Daddy, of course I know how, what do you think I am? But he didn't *do* anything to me, Daddy, he didn't *do* anything to give me a baby."

He believed her. He wanted to believe her. If he called for the doctor, it would be like advertising that she had gone on her back for that damned nigger or—just as bad —that he didn't trust her not to have done it. Therefore he wanted to avoid having the doctor in, if at all possible.

But what did he actually know about Hannah?

No matter what she said, for all he knew she had been getting it since she was twelve and had Chinese twins in the oven right now. For all he knew, she was doomed to be a virgin forever or she was already the parish's richest whore. What did a man ever really know?

He would resist any such barbarity as the castration or the hanging of one of his people, but he didn't really blame Ethan for the violence of his reaction. How was a young blade supposed to behave when he found the girl of his choice alone with another male and both of them stark

28

naked? Never mind the crap about their having been brought up together—they weren't pickaninnies anymore. Tracy was a seventeen-year-old prime hand, good material to put to stud. And Hannah . . . by her own testimony, Hannah was a healthy sixteen-year-old bitch, flagging her tail, whether she realized it or not. Maybe no fornication had taken place before Ethan arrived; but if there had been nothing at all, either human nature had changed a hell of a lot in the last thirty years or something was wrong with both of them.

Addison pulled himself out of his chair. There was no point in putting off the inevitable.

"Do you realize the danger that boy is in?" he asked. "I don't say it's all your fault—he asked for it. But do you realize the danger?"

"But I keep telling you, he didn't do anything!"

"But he did. He got caught with you. And not just a young man with a girl—a nigger with a white girl. Don't you know there'll be people wanting him killed for that? Don't you know what Ethan Flynn tried to do to him? Don't you know that plenty of other men around here would do the same?"

"But he's *Tracy!*" she said, as if that made sense.

"Yes, he's Tracy, and you and Tracy have just about got him lynched unless I can stop it. Since you say you weren't going too far when Ethan and his friends caught you, maybe I can hold it down to a whipping."

She wept. "No. Don't whip him."

"I'm going to have to. And don't say he doesn't deserve a whipping, at the very least, for causing this mess."

"He didn't cause it, Daddy. *I* caused it."

"I suppose you share the responsibility—"

"No, I caused it. I teased him. I made him chase me. I took him away from everybody else so we could be alone. I didn't mean anything bad—I just wanted to play with him like when we were little. Then, when we were alone, I told him I wanted to swim skinny, like we used to. He didn't want to, but I took my shift off anyway, and I teased him for being skirred to take his clothes off too. So finally I got him to take off his clothes, and then we—well, we just *played!* And that's *all!* But it was my fault, and I should get the whipping, not Tracy. Please, Daddy, I *should!*"

Why, the little bitch, he thought, and he felt a surprising touch of pride in her.

"I'm sorry, Hannah, but if it's to be a whipping, Tracy must take it."

"But all of it? Can't I take at least some of it?"

"Do you really want to?"

"Yes!"

"We'll see. I'll bear what you've said in mind."

And now Addison Carter headed for the whipping post.

Tracy knew he wasn't safe yet, and he didn't dare think what might happen next.

"Yes, sir, boy," Simon said, "the minute I heard that girl's voice I came running. And don't you worry, I'm not going away."

"They gon' kill me."

"No, they are not. You didn't hurt that girl, and whatever happens now, it is *not* going to be the worst. Trust me. Trust Simon."

He tried to trust Simon; he always had trusted him. Simon had taught him to read, to calculate, even to speak properly. Simon, as everyone knew, was the smartest black on the plantation. He was even smarter than the overseer and his assistant, and some said he was as smart as Mr. Carter. He read books from the master's library, and he even had books of his own. His two-room cottage was more beautiful and pleasant than the overseer's house, and he had allowed Tracy, who usually slept in a bunk-house, to spend many a night with him. Some said that Simon took a special interest in Tracy because he was the boy's father. Tracy didn't know—he couldn't even remember his dead mother—and he didn't really care. The only thing he knew and cared about was that Simon was his friend, the best he had in the world.

He lay naked on Simon's bed, and the majordomo rubbed whiskey into his wounds. For some reason, this tended to reduce the chances of suppurations and fever and the dreaded lockjaw. In this land, every scratch was a threat to life, and until every single wound on Tracy's body healed, he was in very real danger of losing his life.

"Now, are you sure you've learned your lesson, boy?" Simon asked gently.

"I'm black," Tracy managed to say.

"That's right. What else?"

"I'm a slave."

"And what does that mean?"

Tracy couldn't answer.

"It means that no matter how smart you are, no matter how much they let you learn from books, no matter how much more civilized you are than *they* are—*you are theirs*. And you never, never touch their women."

But you do, Simon.

Tracy had heard Simon talk boldly to white people before, but never as he had today. He had seen other blacks —grown men—being ordered about by small children. But not Simon. The rules that were made for slaves simply didn't apply to the majordomo, and perhaps that was one reason Tracy had taken the older man for his model. He didn't want to be just another field nigger or stable nigger or house lackey. He wanted to be like Simon.

Why, Simon was almost like a free man!

"Like a free man?" Simon laughed quietly and bitterly, and Tracy realized that he must have spoken aloud. "Like a free man, you say! Boy, why do you think I drink? Why do you think that every six months or so I get so drunk I try to tear the world apart?"

It was true: there were times when Simon went smashing through the slave quarters like an angel of death and destruction. One year, when the overseer had built five flimsy huts, much less substantial than the other slave houses, and moreover had allowed all five to get completely out of repair, Simon had gotten drunk and had literally torn all five apart with his bare hands. Nothing had happened to Simon; he hadn't even been whipped.

Tracy said now, "Mr. Carter don't whip you."

"Because he's not a fool, *not* because I'm free! Because I'm the best he's got, the best he owns, the best *slave!*" Simon's voice took on an unusual harshness. "Because he's got me to run his household and check on his overseer and keep an eye on his accountants and God knows what else, and he doesn't want to spoil all that! Because he knows that if he ever lays a whip on me, he'd better kill me, because I just might take it into my head to kill *him* and burn the whole goddam place down! . . . *But not because I'm free!"*

Tracy listened with something like amazement. Simon had never before spoken to him quite like this. And Tracy, born in captivity and raised in it for seventeen years, felt that for the first time he was learning what slavery—and freedom—meant. How could you know what one meant if you had never experienced the other? or if no one really tried to tell you?

He knew, of course, that field hands lived under the severest kind of discipline, but he was not a field hand. He knew that many slaves were horribly overworked, but he never had been. Injustice, brutality, and lynching threatened every black, and Tracy knew many instances of them, but they had never come truly close to him. Until today.

He had never missed a meal in his life. He had never lacked adequate clothing. He was a slave, but comparatively few slaves lived better than he did. He would never have dreamed of trading his slavery for the sordid life of many a poor white he had seen, and he had always assumed that Simon felt the same way. Until now.

"You could run away," he suggested after a moment. Some slaves, he knew, did make successful escapes.

Simon laughed again. "Run where? To the North, Canada, Africa, Europe? And spend the rest of my life feeling guilty for deserting those that need me? Don't you understand, boy, that Addison Carter isn't the only one here that needs me? These are *my* people on this plantation, not Addison Carter's, and *they* need me. *You* need me. I'm one of the strong ones, and there are times when only I can help. You may get a whipping yet, but where'd you be right now if I had run away?"

Tracy was afraid to answer. Simon's bitter rage was growing. The big man paced back and forth by the bed, his fists hard against his forehead. "Jesus Christ, don't you think I *want* to run away? But I tell you this, boy, and my curse on you if you ever forget it. As long as any one man in this world is a slave, no man is free. He may not know it, he may not want it, he may be afraid to admit it—but *no man is free!* And that is not just some kind of Bible talk, Tracy—that is the Godawful truth that they use to help keep us trapped!"

Simon collapsed into a chair and buried his face in his big hands. "Christ, I need a drink," he mumbled after a minute.

The cottage was silent.

"Simon."

Tracy recognized Mr. Carter's voice, and a stroke of fear went through him. His body tensed, and he drew up his knees as if to hide himself. Simon stood up and went into the other room without giving Tracy a look. Tracy imagined that Mr. Carter was standing right outside the door.

"Mr. Add," he heard Simon say quietly, "you're not going to let them burn or brand or cut that boy."

"Of course not, Simon. But he is going to have to take a whipping. I hope you understand."

"Is it really necessary? Hasn't he been punished enough? Mr. Add, I don't know if you noticed how badly that boy was cut up, and he's been frightened out of his wits—"

"Who's giving the orders around here, Mr. Carter," a third voice—Follett's—said, "you or this nigger? He don't like it, we can always take his balls off, too—"

"That's enough," Mr. Carter said calmly. "Either keep your filthy mouth shut or get off my land." Then, "It is necessary, Simon. Please bring Tracy out."

If Simon said "Yes, sir," Tracy didn't hear it. The majordomo appeared at the door, and Tracy forced himself to rise from the bed without help, though he had all he could do to keep from sobbing. He found that his legs still shook; they would barely support him. Simon started to hold out a hand, then saw that Tracy didn't want it.

Every step took effort, and he thought he might fall at any moment, but he forced himself to walk through the cottage, through the door, and down the three steps to the ground. A path opened before him—Ethan Flynn and his friends, as well as Mr. Carter, the overseer and his assistant, and a number of slaves were in the crowd—and once again his sheer nakedness felt horrible.

The post was not far, but it seemed to take all the strength he had, and with each step, his fear grew. He wanted to weep like a child. *Don't do this to me. Please don't do this to me. Please don't whip me. I'll be good. Oh, please, please* . . . He knew that the only reason he didn't cry was that Simon was beside him.

Through blurred eyes, he saw that all the other slaves had been gathered at the post. They were all there to see his fear, his degradation, his pain. The gathering was customary: they were all to learn a lesson.

He was at the post, hardly believing he was already facing the dark, weathered wood.

"Put out your hands," the assistant overseer said. He was a young man named Tom Barclay, and he performed his task with the quickness and indifference of an expert. He wrapped rags around Tracy's wrists to protect them, then bound them together with leather thongs. He made Tracy lift his hands over his head and tied the thongs to an iron ring attached to the post. Next he hobbled Tracy, then he fastened his knees so that he couldn't throw his body too far from the post or with too great force against it. He stepped back.

Tracy braced himself, but the time had not yet come. First Mr. Carter had to explain to the witnesses why this whipping was taking place.

"Maybe you all think you already know why this boy is being whipped. Maybe you think he's gone and done some terrible crime. Maybe you think this is just the beginning and he's going to lose all he's got and all he ever had and all he might have had. Well, you're wrong. This is a good boy. This is one of the best boys I've ever known, and he's going to have a long and happy life. They just don't come no finer than this here boy.

"Then, you may ask, why is he being whipped? I'll tell you why. Because he broke a rule you all know about. That rule is, don't ever let anybody think you *might* have done something bad or *could* have done something bad. That rule is, don't never do nothing that *might* bring disgrace on a Carter nigger. Don't ever let anyone *suspect* you of being anything but a good nigger.

"Now, I say again, this is a good nigger. I don't want to hear anyone saying otherwise. I hear anything like that from any of you, I'll put you to the post so fast you won't know what happened."

Tracy heard Mr. Carter's feet shuffling in the dust as he stepped away. He saw Aaron Wills, the overseer, examining several whips. The sun was lowering now, but the day was still bright and hot. "No, goddammit," Mr. Carter said, "not the rawhide, just an ordinary short field whip." Tracy saw Ethan Flynn sucking on a blade of grass. Ethan wasn't smiling now.

"Give him twenty-five, to start," Mr. Carter murmured.

"All right," Wills said, "stand back." And the whip whisked through the air.

And landed on Tracy's shoulder blades.

He had no idea when he began to scream. He seemed to be dissolving in explosions of fire that never stopped burning. His body, his soul, the entire world was turning to fire. Nothing was worth what he was going through today, nothing was worth this. How could he ever have thought that he loved Hannah—but he had, but he did—no, no, she meant nothing to him, he would never look at her again, he would do only what they wanted him to do, be only what they wanted him to be, but stop it, oh please master make him stop, I just a nigger, I just a nigger slave, I a nothing, nothing, nothing, nothing, but oh please stop ... please ... please. ...

"That's enough."

"Only eighteen, Mr. Carter—seven left to go."

"No point in whipping him when he's unconscious."

"We can bring him back again—"

"I said, that's enough. Give me that whip. You and Tom untie him."

"Shit," one of the Colbys said, "didn't even break the skin."

"Well, boys," Ethan said, "you all heard Mr. Carter—this here is a *good* nigger."

"You can go home now," Addison told him. "Simon, where do you want the boy taken?"

"Just give him to me. I'll take him to my cottage. I'll take care of him."

"You heard that, Mr. Wills?"

"Yes, sir."

Whip in hand, Addison headed back toward the big house. Though he had remained as stoic as possible, he felt drained; and the episode was far from over. Before entering the house, he paused for a moment and looked toward the majordomo's cottage. Simon was carrying the unconscious boy in his arms like a child.

He found his sister Rachel in the pantry. She was weeping, apparently having watched or heard the whipping from the window. Still handsome, Addison thought; even beautiful. Auburn hair and eyes as blue as Hannah's. Good bones in her face, a good body. Widowed. Life had cheated her and, though she didn't yet know it, it was about to cheat her again.

Women, he thought. *Southern* women! Either they were colder than ice, or they couldn't keep their drawers up for an hour. The cold ones regarded all men as dirty chasers of nigger wenches, and the rutty ones would stop at nothing to get what they wanted. And you couldn't always tell which would turn out to be which. The one who led you on might wind up insulted and indignant, while the one who shivered with fear when you touched her elbow might beg you until at last you took her.

"Crying won't help," he said.

"I know."

"Do you know whose fault this is? Not Tracy's, not Hannah's—ours. *Our* fault, Rachel."

"I told you not to let her run wild, but you insisted—"

"I think you're right, I have been lax. I wanted her to run wild, I wanted her to grow up in the yard and the quarters and the fields. I wanted her to grow up with other children, black and white, and not become one of these prissy, housebound, constipated Southern white females. I still think I was right, but we should have watched her more closely—"

"I tried to watch her Addison!"

"And I suppose I discouraged you. But what kind of example were *you* giving her?"

Rachel stared at him, and he couldn't help feeling sorry for her.

"I . . . I'm not sure I know what you mean," she said.

"Oh, come, Rachel! Rachel and Simon, Hannah and Tracy. The equation is obvious, isn't it?"

Rachel looked bewildered. "Simon and I . . ."

"Rachel, everybody on this plantation must know about you and Simon, and you must know that everybody knows. We just don't talk about it, that's all. And our people don't dare talk about it. And they think enough of Simon that they don't want to talk about it. But do you really think that Hannah doesn't know?"

"Oh, God." Rachel hid her face.

Addison sighed. He really didn't want to hurt his sister, but he knew he was going to have to. For the moment, he contented himself with saying, "Something's got to be done, Rachel. A whipping or two isn't the solution. Something drastic has got to be done."

He weighed the whip in his hand thoughtfully, and he shook his head. He left the pantry and went up the back stairs.

From her room Hannah couldn't hear the whip, but she could hear Tracy scream: the first scream, the second scream, the third, and before long the scream that never really stopped until the whipping was over. She lay face down on her bed and dug her fingers and her teeth into her pillow and tried to keep from screaming herself.

She had thought she had learned what a whipping was. She had seen the snakes crack out at black legs and shoulders in the fields, and she had, like most children, been thrashed herself. She had even known of other slaves to go to the post. But this whipping was different. This whipping was for Tracy, and it was her fault, and it hurt.

She knew, when she thought about it, that a great many white people scorned and hated blacks. She knew that they frequently whipped, tortured, and killed blacks. She had heard her father express loathing and contempt for the kind of master who would geld a slave, so she was aware that such things did happen. She remembered nights when the slaves maintained a frightened quiet in their quarters because something terrible was happening in the town, but she never really understood why her father wouldn't let her go see the "black meat hanging from the trees" the next day. For years she had no real idea of what the phrase meant. She had been a pickaninny among black pickaninnies, learning from them the difference between little girls and little boys long before she learned the difference between black and white, slave and free.

Now she was learning.

Now, just turned sixteen, she was bursting out of her cocoon of innocence. For the first time she realized that she and Tracy were expected to live in different worlds and that the penalty for trying to bring the two worlds together could be painful beyond belief.

The fact that her Aunt Rachel and Simon had thus far escaped punishment meant nothing: Tracy was now being whipped. And this was not the worst that could have happened. The moment Ethan and his friends had appeared, a sense of reality had begun to infect Hannah like a disease. Other children, like Ethan, had known the difference between black and white, slave and free, as if from birth; and she *knew* that Ethan and the others meant to castrate and murder Tracy. She knew that the fright-tales of torturing and killing "bad niggers" and feeding them to the hogs were not simply obscene jokes. She also knew that she was responsible for what was happening.

When the screaming stopped, she took a long shuddering breath. Slowly she relaxed. She waited.

She seemed to be drifting into sleep when she heard the knock at the door. She was sure it was her father and guessed why he was here. She told him to come in.

When she heard the door open and close again, she looked over her shoulder and saw the whip in her father's hand, and she closed her eyes tightly. Fear was growing into something like terror.

"I had Mr. Wills give him a set of twenty-five," her father said. "I was going to sentence him to another twenty-five, but I think he's had enough. He lost consciousness

38

after eighteen lashes, which means he still has seven to collect."

Hannah said nothing. She kept her eyes tightly closed. She wanted to say, *Give the seven to me instead,* but she couldn't.

"Did you mean what you said about sharing Tracy's punishment?" her father asked.

She forced herself to say "Yes."

"Then get off the bed. Stand by the bedpost."

She opened her eyes and climbed off the bed. Her legs shook, and she wondered if Tracy's had shaken too.

"Hold the bedpost as tightly as you can," her father said. "You might find it easier if I tied your wrists."

"No."

She gripped the post. This couldn't be too bad, she thought, looking for courage. Other girls had been whipped and were none the worse for it. She herself had been caned and switched a number of times, and this couldn't be *too* different. And she was only going to take seven lashes, while Tracy had taken eighteen.

Her father lifted her shift, pulled it over her head, and let it hang down from her elbows. She hadn't expected that, and a painful sob tore from her throat.

"Hannah," her father said thickly, "you deserve this and much more, but I don't really want to do it—"

"Do it!" she cried. "All seven—I don't care! But do it!"

It was far worse than she had expected, this baptism of the whip; and when it was over, she was no longer a girl. She was a woman.

chapter three

Tracy awakened to pain and sank back into darkness, and pain and darkness became a cycle. In time, there seemed to be a little less of each, a little less pain, then a little less darkness, but the pain continued. Once, he became aware that Simon was leaning over him, doing something to his back. Later, he became aware that he was once more on Simon's bed, still naked, lying face down. Then darkness came again.

When he awakened, it was daylight, but he couldn't have said if it were morning or evening or if the whipping had taken place two hours or two days before. He stayed close to sleep as if afraid to get too far from it.

"Simon?"

"Yes, boy?"

"Are you there?"

Somewhere in the room Simon laughed. "Of course I'm here. I'm sorry I woke you up."

"Is it over?"

"It's all over, boy."

He didn't know if he drifted back into sleep then for another hour or another day.

"Simon?"

"Yes, boy."

"How many . . . how many did Mr. Wills give me?"

"Eighteen. You did fine."

"I screamed, I couldn't help it."

"You did fine. Those white trash wanted you to fall to you knees and blubber like a baby. You didn't. You walked like a man."

"My legs shook."

"You walked like a man," Simon repeated, and Tracy noticed the slurring in his voice. Simon was drinking.

Tracy tried to think. "The master said twenty-five."

"There's not going to be any more, boy. I told you that. Believe me."

"But didn't you say Mr. Wills only gave me eighteen?"

"That's right. He stopped when you passed out."

"Then I still got seven coming."

"I told you, no more. It's over."

"But—"

"Someone else took them for you."

"For me? Who? Not you, Simon?"

Simon's choked laugh told Tracy that the majordomo had drunk far more than he would otherwise have suspected. "No. Not me. Your paramour, Mr. Tracy. From now on, I want you to call her Miss Hannah."

"Hannah?"

"Miss Hannah. The little bitch should have taken them all, but I guess you deserve what you got, for being such a fool. She'll turn out to be like every other white bitch, I guess, but for a little girl, she's got a nice tough streak of nigger in her somewhere. . . . Like her aunt."

"You mean she didn't have to take them?"

"Not from what Mr. Add tells me. And whatever he may be, I never took him for a liar."

Tracy tried to comprehend Hannah's taking seven lashes for him, but for the moment his mind and imagination were too weak. He found himself floating back into darkness.

And then someone was weeping.

How long the weeping went on he had no idea, but it seemed to go on forever, as he hovered near the edge of his darkness. Gradually he moved closer to it, and he realized it came from a woman. Hannah? No, but some woman he knew. . . .

Aunt Rachel . . .

"He won't change his mind."

She was in the other room. This was Simon's bedroom, he realized, and he was lying on Simon's bed. It was night. And Hannah's Aunt Rachel was in the other room. . . .

"When do you leave, Rachel?"

"Within the week."

"You'll be back."

"But not for at least four years. Four years, Simon. We could be dead in four years. We're not young, Simon— even if we live, in four years I'll be old. You won't want me anymore—"

"I'll always want you."

"Don't let him send me away. Please don't let him send me away—"

"For God's sake, woman, don't tell *me* to stop him! I'm a bondman, remember? I'm a nigger, a black, a darkie, a slave! It's partly because of *me* that he's sending you and Hannah away!"

Hannah . . . Hannah going away . . .

And Aunt Rachel weeping as if her heart was breaking. He had heard black women weep that way when their children died, but somehow it had never occurred to him that Aunt Rachel could weep like a black woman.

"I can't exist without you," Aunt Rachel said.

"Can't exist," Simon said angrily. "Christ, woman, at least expect as much from yourself as you do from some old nigger bitch!"

"I *am* an old nigger bitch. Don't throw my whiteness at me."

"I'm sorry. I'm sorry. I love you."

Time passed. Perhaps hours.

"Simon . . . the boy . . ."

"He's asleep."

"You're sure?"

"Yes."

"Oh, God . . . how can I live . . . without you . . . without this."

"Don't."

"At least I won't have to worry anymore about having a black baby, will I—"

"Stop it, Rachel! Please!"

"I'm sorry, my darling. I won't spoil it. I promise."

"I love you, I love you."

"Forever?"

"Now, now, now!"

"Now, darling . . . Now . . ."

Tracy awoke to full daylight and the sound of activity outside the cottage. He called Simon, but got no answer. His entire body was painfully stiff, and he ached terribly, but the worst of the agony seemed to be over. He remembered talking to Simon and hearing Simon talk to Aunt Rachel, but he couldn't be sure that he hadn't dreamed the conversations.

With some difficulty, he managed to sit up on the edge of the bed. His mouth was uncomfortably dry, and his eyes felt swollen with sleep. He looked around the room, hoping to see some clothes he could put on.

He was still sitting on the edge of the bed five minutes later, when Simon entered the cottage carrying pants, shirt, and brogans. Simon was wearing his livery: Mr. Carter fancied white gloves and embroidered white vests for his majordomo. He smiled and said, "So you're up and with us again." Tracy smelled whiskey.

"How long have I been here?"

"The better part of two days. You slept most of the time, but you did wake up and talk to me. Don't you remember?"

"A little bit."

"How do you feel?"

"I ache. I ache worse than I ever did in my whole life."

"Ever did *before*," Simon corrected him. "Are you hungry?"

Suddenly Tracy was ravenous; it must have shown on his face, because Simon laughed and said, "It's almost noon; we'll get you something to eat. You rest easy this afternoon, and tonight you're going to move back to your own bed. I'm tired of doing without mine."

He tossed the clothes onto the bed beside Tracy, and Tracy noticed that they weren't house clothes.

"Ain't I gon' work in the house?"

This time Simon didn't bother to correct him. When he spoke, there was a huskiness in his voice. "No, you're going to work in the stables for the next few days. You're going to work there until Miss Hannah is gone."

"Gone?" He searched his memory; he had heard something. . . .

"In a few days she's leaving for Europe. Her Aunt Rachel will accompany her as her governess and chaperon. They'll tour the Continent, and Miss Hannah will receive an education appropriate to a young lady of her station. Do you understand all these book words, Tracy? They will be gone at least four years, and on return, Miss Hannah will no doubt marry some suitable young man, such as Mr. Ethan Flynn. It is then fervently to be hoped that, having been subjected to a foreign atmosphere for a number of years, she will at last be beyond the carnal temptations of hard young nigger flesh. . . ."

Simon collapsed into a chair. He slumped. His fingers drifted across his eyes, and Tracy couldn't read the expression on his face. When he continued speaking, his voice shook in a way that Tracy had never heard before, and it took on the accents of the cane fields.

"And her aunt, too. Oh, yes, Miz Rachel, too. She, too, must be placed beyond temptation. For the sake of all we hold dear, dear Lord. Lord, Lord, lead us not into temptation. Ne'er you mind the black ladies, Lord, you just keep you eye on the white cunt. Yes, and on all the black studs that threaten their chastity. Forget all those black wenches, Lord—Lord, we all know they are meant to breed. 'Cause how we gon' have field hands if'n they don't breed, Lord? How we gon' have nigger babies to sell?

"Send white men among us to guide us in thy path, Lord. Send white men among us to teach us thy righteousness.

"And then deliver us from evil, Lord. Just You try. . . ."

Tracy stared.

The slave quarters on the Carter Louisiana plantation consisted largely of two-family tenements and individual two- and three-room houses. There were also a number of one-room cabins, occupied by single blacks, but most single men and women without families lived in bunkhouses. It was to one of these that Tracy returned when he left Simon's cottage.

He was well enough liked, but he had few real friends. He was a house nigger, and the majority of the men he lived with were field hands; they begrudgingly granted him a special status but resented him. His clothes were better than theirs, he talked differently, and his work was generally lighter and cleaner. Still, Tracy frequently got his hands dirty in the stables, and he had been whipped for doing the most dangerous thing a black man could do: he had messed around with a white female. His acquaintances hardly knew whether to regard him as a fool or a hero, but in any case, they looked on him with a certain amount of awe.

"Tracy, Master never do say zactly what you do. What you do, boy, you cotch you such a floggin'?"

They all seemed to be waiting for him—Bardo, Kemp, Darius, Florian—when he returned to his quarters that evening. Tracy didn't want to talk about the episode.

"I didn't do nothing."

"Shit, everybody know what he done. He been puttin' his nigger pecker in Miz Hannah, is what."

"Aw, he never did! You don't get no floggin', you do that! Leastways, you get lots worse afterwards!"

"I still think he done it—"

"You better not say it, boy, or you gon' get worse than he got. Master set that Mr. Ethan Flynn on you, and no Simon gon' call him off!"

"You gon' tell on me?"

"You talk too much, somebody hear, that's all."

"That true, Tracy? 'Bout how Mr. Ethan try to cut you up, and Simon make him stop?"

"That's true."

"Then must be true Mr. Ethan cotch you bareass nekkid with Miz Hannah. How you like that white meat, Tracy?"

"Don't ask Tracy. Ask Simon. *He* know."

"Jesus, you all keep talking so free and easy like this, you gon' get us *all* whipped!"

"That Simon, he something wonderful."

"Gettin' drunk again."

"Blowin' up a storm."

" 'Member last time?"

"Half bear and half gator."

"Half hurry-cane, half fire!"

"And you know why?"

"Master's sending his woman across the seas, is why. No more Miz Rachel in Simon's bed, is why."

"All right, keep talkin'! Get us all killed! Go on!"

"Tracy, you still ain't tell us zactly what you and Miz Hannah done."

"Didn't do nothin'," Tracy said impatiently. "Just went swimmin' with Hannah like I been doin' since I a pickaninny. Then that Ethan and the Colbys and some others found us, and I guess Ethan lookin' to find himself some fun. So he took exception to my swimming with a white girl, say I too old for that, and he and his friends pull off my pants and chase me all around. They poke me with them pig-stickers and slash at me and finally get me down on my back. Then Simon come and stop 'em."

"You mean you don't go swimmin' in your birthday suit with that gal?"

"Course not. You think I crazy?"

"Then how it happen Miz Hannah come runnin' home all screamin' and bareass nekkid?"

"Boy, how do I know? I got enough worries 'bout hanging onto my pecker without worrying how some white gal done lost her shift!"

The others burst out laughing and turned away, and Tracy saw that, for the time being at least, their curiosity was satisfied. Left alone, he stretched out on his bed. Though his body was still a vessel of pain, the actual whipping and the events that had preceded it now seemed distant and dreamlike. When he mentioned the attempted castration, the thought still held terror, and he had all he

46

could do to keep from clutching at his groin; yet he could hardly believe the incident had actually taken place, it had such a strange quality in his mind. And when he thought of Hannah, he could hardly believe that they had actually held each other and kissed. How had he ever thought that he loved her? He didn't feel now that he could ever love anyone: it was almost as if Simon hadn't arrived in time, and he had been castrated after all. Neither Hannah nor any other woman was worth what had happened to him.

The white people had taught him his lesson.

Women!

Addison wandered through the unilluminated gloom of his house in the evening and cursed them. Hannah went about in a daze and acted as if she couldn't quite understand what had happened or what was about to happen. At least she showed no signs of hating him; if anything, the contrary: there were little signs of affection he had not noticed before, and at times, they almost broke his heart.

And Rachel. Damned woman, red-eyed and shaky-voiced every time you spoke to her. Couldn't say he blamed her, but she acted as if she had the female complaint on top of everything else. He would be glad when the next two days had passed. Then he would be shed of the two women and could live in peace.

No, that wasn't true. He would miss both of them, he would miss them terribly. And he couldn't be sure he would see either of them again—neither he nor Rachel was young. He'd already seen at least half of his generation into the grave. . . . He wondered why the hell he was sending Hannah and Rachel away.

But there was no help for it. Hannah had been raised too close to the blacks, he saw that now—and in this world, that just didn't work. She had to be sent away until she had more reason, more discretion. Anyway, he'd long contemplated sending her abroad to complete her education, so this constituted no great change of plans.

She couldn't go alone; she had turned sixteen, but she was still, in many ways, too much a child. The incident with Tracy demonstrated that, even if it did nothing else. She needed someone to look after her, and he had no relatives in England whom he considered to be close enough, even if they were willing. Besides, Hannah would be traveling about the Continent a great deal. Yes, she would need Rachel, and where Hannah was concerned, both Rachel and he could damned well make sacrifices; they could try to make up for the harm they had done her.

He wandered out in back of the big white house. The sun was down now, but the air was still hot and muggy. A mosquito whined, and Addison slapped at his cheek. Like most sugar plantations, this one lay close to the swamps. He thanked God that fevers weren't too bad this year. He had known them to carry off many a slave. And one year, Hannah's mother.

He lit a cigar and looked about. There were a few lights in the slave quarters. He liked to think that he treated his people well, damned well, and that the more intelligent among them appreciated the fact. Which brought Simon to mind . . .

Addison looked toward Simon's cottage, saw no signs of life. Nevertheless, he strolled toward it. Damned nigger, he'd been drinking again since the day Tracy was whipped, and each day he was a little drunker. The last couple of days he hadn't even made a pretense of being sober, hadn't appeared at the house to do his work, hadn't done anything but set a bad example for the other blacks. Wills, the overseer, wanted to whip him, but Wills was almost as big a fool about house niggers as he was wise about field hands. And jealous of Simon to boot. Addison had to admit to himself that he found the idea of having Simon whipped rather frightening.

When he reached the cottage, he found Simon sitting in the darkness of the open doorway, a jug at his side. Simon made no attempt to hide it, nor did he stand up as was expected of him. He merely glanced at Addison and said nothing. Addison felt a bitter sympathy.

"Mind if I take a swallow of your jug, Simon?"

"Suit yourself. It's your whiskey."

Addison forced himself to laugh. "Yes, I suppose it is."

"Like everything else 'round here." Simon said bitterly.

"Oh, I wouldn't say that. There are quite a few things around here that aren't mine. Like your books, for instance, the ones I've given you and the ones you've acquired on your own—"

"Do I get to fight to keep 'em?"

"What?" Simon's speech was slurred. Addison took a fiery sip from the jug and set it down again.

"I said, can I keep you from taking 'em back? Do I get to fight to keep 'em."

"Well, no, but we all have certain things that could be taken—"

"Then they ain't mine."

Addison felt that Simon was being unreasonable. "Simon, everything we have in this world we have only on sufferance. Not only you, but I too—"

"Who owns you, Mr. Add?"

"God is the Father of us all," Addison said patiently.

"No, who *owns* you, who *owns* you? Who buys and sells your body—"

"I have never trafficked in slaves, as you well know. I have purchased slaves, but they have found homes here—"

"No, that's not the question, Mr. Add! *Who—owns you?*"

Addison sighed. Life would have been a good deal simpler in some respects if he hadn't liked, in some ways even admired, Simon. Simon might put on the accents of a field hand, but he was nothing of the sort; he was an intelligent, educated, and civilized human being. Addison had even dared to say aloud that he respected Simon far more than certain whites he had met.

"I suppose it must all seem very unfair to you," he said.

Simon, sipping from the jug, exploded in smothered drunken laughter. Addison ignored that and went on speaking. "But the sad fact is that from time immemorial the highest civilizations have been built on some form of slavery. And to be a slave is not necessarily a disgrace. Some of the noblest figures of antiquity have been slaves—"

"Mr. Add, sir, beggin' yo' pardon, sir, I just a ole black boy, sir, I ain't concerned with no noble figure of antiquity. Do you honest-to-God believe what you talkin' 'bout got anything to do with the nekkid black flesh and the slavemongerin' and the whippin' and the hangin', with sellin' babies out'n their mothers' arms and geldin' men and boys and settin' 'em on fire with coal oil, with workin' them to death and starvin' them to death, and layin' with their wives and daughters, then whippin' their wives and daughters nekkid at the post before they own husbands' and chillun's eyes—"

"Stop that nigger talk, Simon—you know I don't do that—"

"I *am* a nigger, Mr. Add, sir, and what you mean you don't do it? I *seen* you have a woman whipped nekkid before her family—"

"There were special circumstances—"

"And now you say you don't do that, like you don't even *'member,* Mr. Add, sir! And just few days ago, you take poor Tracy, him scared sick of being cut up, you take him nekkid to the post and you—"

"And I probably saved his life! I *had* to do it, Simon—"

"That's right, sir. You had to do it. 'Cause you're part of it. . . . But, now, you'n me, we're different, ain't we, sir? You'n me, we always been able to talk to each other like two human beings, ain't we, sir?"

"I've always thought so, yes."

"And yet I know that every time I open my mouth and talk to you like this, I takin' a big chance on you havin' my tongue cut out."

"That, bluntly, is a lie."

Simon looked up slyly. "You gettin' mad at Simon, Mr. Add? 'Cause if you get mad enough, you gon' cut my tongue out even while you callin' me a liar. And you want to know why? 'Cause you *can,* that's why, 'cause you *can.* And now I gon' tell you a secret 'bout people, Mr. Add. Those that *can,* if'n they live long enough, sooner or later they *do.*"

"Do you honestly think—"

"It is a possibility which I always bear in mind." Simon's field accent had disappeared abruptly.

"Then no man can trust his friend."

"How much less a slave his master."

Addison slapped at another mosquito and listened to

the night-sounds of insects. He wished Simon would offer him the jug or make some other forgiving gesture; he had had no idea that the black man's bitterness ran so deep. He had thought of the two of them as having a special relationship beyond the bounds of convention. He had recognized the man's intelligence and sensitivity, he had helped him gain an education in a time and place where teaching a black to read was usually regarded as a crime, he had given Simon a life of comfort beyond what most white men could expect . . . and now it was as if all this counted for nothing. Addison had no illusion that Simon's bitterness was caused solely by Rachel's being taken from him.

"I didn't know you hated me," he said after a moment.

"I don't hate you, Mr. Add. At least not twenty-four hours a day. Sometimes I rather like you."

"Thank you. I'm sorry if I seemed to be insulting your intelligence with my remarks about slavery as a basis of civilization. I'm quite aware that the point is not beyond debate. But the fact remains that we find ourselves within our Southern civilization with its peculiar economic needs and its way of life—"

"I know it. I, of all people, know it."

"And there's nothing we can do about it."

"Nothing, Mr. Add? You are one of the richest and most powerful men in the South, and there is *nothing* you can do?"

Addison hesitated. His wealth and power were, after all, based on cane and cotton crops, and those crops were made possible by slave labor.

"Things do change in time," he said at last. "Nothing has ever remained the same."

Simon lowered his head and went back to field-hand accents. "Ole Simon, he gon' take deep comfort from that thought. He gon' 'member that when his people's dyin' in the fields."

"Someone *always* dies in the fields." Having said the words, Addison found himself slightly shocked. He tried to soften their impact. "That is regrettable, but it is a fact. It's simply part of this vale of tears which we must all accept."

"Yes, master."

"I know you're having a particularly trying time at present. But I would like to think that we can go on, in our own way, being friends."

"Our own way. Yes, master."

Addison was not at all sure that he and Simon were speaking the same language. He was not at all sure, now, that they ever had. Without another word, he turned away from the cottage door and walked slowly back to his mansion.

"Well, look like yo' big friend finally got hisself some deep trouble," Isaiah said, grinning, as he entered the stables.

Tracy was worried. He'd been worried about Simon since the majordomo had started his steady drinking. "What he do?"

"You know that big mean driver, Yardley? Simon knock him on his ass. No reason, 'ceptin' Yardley is mean and Simon he feelin' meaner. Simon he just walk up to Yardley and say, 'Yardley, you a mean nigger and I gon' bust yo' head.' Yardley laugh, and *boom!* Simon busts him. Now, Master can't do nothing but let the captain put ole Simon to the post."

"They can't do that to Simon!"

"Ho-ho, you wait!"

"Simon won't let 'em!"

"How he gon' stop 'em?"

"I better go find Simon—"

"Now you stay here, boy!" Tracy tried to run out the door, but Isaiah caught his shirt and held him. "You got one whippin', that is enough. Simon don't need you, you ain't gon' do him no good, and Master say for you to hitch up Pete to the good shay for Miz Rachel. Do it *now!*"

"Do you know where Simon is?"

"He strollin' through the quarters somewhere, looking fo' people to knock on they ass. Don't you worry, they go out 'n cotch him soon, take him to the post, and then *whoo-ee!* That old whip cotch up with Simon at last!"

There were those who envied Simon, and Tracy saw that Isaiah felt a certain satisfaction at the thought that

Simon wasn't beyond the reach of the whip. "Maybe Mr. Carter let Simon and Yardley fight it out."

Isaiah shook his head. "Nothing left of Yardley to do no fightin'. And Simon been drunk almos' a week now. The colonel he *got* to do something about Simon."

Tracy tried to believe otherwise as he went about the business of hitching Pete to the shay, but it was difficult. For the last day or so, Simon had been like a mad man. He had hardly seemed to know Tracy. He had staggered about the quarters, often carrying a jug on his shoulder, babbling incoherently, sometimes howling like an enraged animal. Any other slave would have been whipped and locked up long before now. Only because Simon was a very special person on the plantation had he gone unpunished.

Tracy, leading Pete to the shay, paused as he heard distant laughter, a loud whoop that could only have been Simon, and then more laughter from Simon's audience. Isaiah looked around and grinned.

"That ole boy truly 'joyin' hisself. Long's he gon' cotch it anyway, he figure he gon' have hisself a time. . . . You get done there, you help me mule-up some wagons."

Isaiah left, and Tracy was glad to be alone. He realized that there was really nothing he could do for Simon, and he hated listening to Isaiah's remarks about the punishment coming to the majordomo. As he finished hitching up Pete, he looked out of the stable and across the yard and saw Hannah coming out of the house. She was dressed up as if she might be going into town. He had seen her at a distance two or three times in the last few days, but their eyes had never met, and he had had no desire to speak to her. She was nothing to him now other than a reminder of pain and humiliation. And yet he stood still and watched as she walked toward him through the hot sunlight; he stood there and waited, his heart beginning to thump, when he could have hurried away.

She came to the door of the stable and hesitated for a moment, pulling at the wide brim of her bonnet.

"Hey, there," she said, and once again he was struck by the blueness of her eyes. She seemed unsure as to whether she should smile at him or not. She stepped into the stable.

"Afternoon," he said.

"You got ole Pete ready for Aunt Rachel and me?"

"Sho'nough. See for yourself."

She glanced at the horse and shay not really seeing them, then she looked again at Tracy. She tried to smile.

"You mad at me for getting you in trouble, Tracy?"

"No, I ain't mad."

"I'm glad. 'Cause I guess you know I'm going away for four, five years starting tomorrow, and I sure don't want to spend the next four or five years thinking, 'How am I gon' get that goddam Tracy over being mad at me?' "

Suddenly his indifference toward her vanished. It was as if a dam had broken and let all of his most tender feelings rush toward her, and he had to laugh. It was a very shaky laugh but a real one.

"You know I ain't mad! I told you how I—how I—how I feel—"

"You said you love me."

She grinned at him. Her grin was broad and slightly crooked with a touch of totally innocent lewdness about it, and they both burst out laughing.

"We sure cotch it good," she said. "That damn Ethan, he skirred the piss out of me!"

"You think *you* skirred!"

"Whoo-ee, I know! I get skirred thinking about it now!"

"If it hadn't been you got Simon there just in time—"

"Oh, don't say it, Tracy—"

"If he got there just about five watch-ticks later—"

"Don't say it, I gon' puke!"

"Not in *my* stable, you ain't!"

They both laughed until tears came to their eyes.

"Poor Tracy," she said when she could speak again. "You went and got yourself whipped, and it was all my fault."

"Wasn't neither. Besides, I hear how you take some of the whipping for me." He had given little thought to the fact that they had shared the punishment, but now the sharing was important. "And I thank you."

"Was only seven lashes."

"But they hurt."

"Oh, sure. My ole daddy, he do know how to lay it on. And I guess I wasn't brave the way you were."

"I wasn't brave! All the way to the post, my legs shake like cane in a high wind!"

"But you walked by yourself—"

"And then *yell?* Didn't you hear me *yell?* I mean to tell you I *yelled*—"

"You yelled! Listen, you should have heard *me* yell! I mean I howled my damn head off—"

"Aw, listen—"

"Nobody can yell like me when I set my mind to it! I'm a girl!"

They laughed more quietly now, and she took both of his hands in hers.

"I guess maybe this is the last chance I'll have to talk to you alone before Aunt Rachel and me go to Europe."

"I reckon."

She looked down at the floor. "And I guess the next time I see you, you'll have some nice black gal for a wife and a whole throng of pickaninnies coming up."

"Maybe so."

"But you won't forget all the fun we had, will you?"

"Course I won't, not ever."

" 'Cause I'll never forget. I'll remember everything good we ever done from the time we was little babies till the time you told me I was beautiful and you loved me. I'm gon' remember how we went swimming and how we kissed. And I'm gon' remember that I loved you, too."

She pulled the brim of her hat aside and kissed his cheek. She stepped away from him and forced a smile. Her voice was overly bright: "And now I guess I'll just mosey off to Europe and learn to be a lady—"

A scream interrupted their talk.

Other voices, raised in fear, were not far away. Tracy and Hannah stared at each other.

Simon, he thought.

People were shouting. There was an explosive sound and the rending of wood, as if something were being torn apart. Tracy had no idea what.

Warnings were shouted: *"Look out!" "Stay away!" "Don't get near!"*

Hannah said, "What in tarnation is going on out there!" and started out the door. Tracy grabbed her wrist and said, "Don't go!"

The voices were suddenly outside the stable, though Tracy and Hannah could see no one from where they stood. Isaiah, sweating and panting, ran in through the door. "That friend of yours, he sho gon' get it now," he said. "He done had his day, that nigger. He diggin' hisself a real grave, the way he carryin' on—"

Hannah let out a yell, and Tracy looked around. Simon had entered through the back of the stable and was swinging an ax around his head as he ran into the room. His eyes bulged with an insane fury. Tracy called his name, but he showed no sign of hearing.

He swung the ax low, and it smashed broadside into Isaiah's leg. There was a sound like snapping kindling, and the man screamed and fell to the floor. Still screaming, he tried to drag himself away from Simon. Simon raised the ax again and swung it as Hannah started toward the door. He hit the horse, Pete, squarely in the forehead, and the animal fell dead. Hannah turned to run as she saw what had happened, but she tripped and fell over Isaiah. She saw Simon glaring blindly at her, saw him raising the bloody ax over his head, and like Isaiah she screamed and tried to drag herself away.

Tracy would never know how the pitchfork came to his hands. He knew only that it was in his hands and that Simon was raising the ax and that in the next instant the ax would almost certainly descend on Hannah.

The next thing he knew was that he was thrusting the fork with all his strength, thrusting it forward and up, driving the tines as deep as they would go, driving them into Simon's great chest.

chapter four

He was too shocked to feel grief. He lay on his bed, and when others tried to talk to him about what had happened, he hardly heard them. Mr. Wills came to question him, and he forgot to stand up and had no idea of what to say. Wills arrived angry and departed angrier. In a little while, the others left him alone.

The dinner hour came. The hands came in from the fields. The bunkhouse foreman tried to persuade Tracy to go eat, but he failed. When he offered to bring food back, Tracy shook his head.

Simon was dead. He couldn't quite believe that, couldn't quite understand it. *What had happened?* Why had Simon hurt people, killed the horse, raised the ax over Hannah's head? Had Simon really done these things? Or was this all part of the terrible nightmare that had begun a week ago when Ethan and his friends had tried to mutilate him?

Wills came back and made Tracy follow him out of the bunkhouse; Tracy, still in a daze, went meekly. They went to a large open-sided shed generally used to issue orders to the drivers, and there Mr. Carter awaited them. Mr.

Carter sat in a chair, and a great number of blacks stood nearby, waiting and listening.

"All right, Tracy," Mr. Carter said gently, "do you think you can tell us about it now?"

Tracy told what he could, as Mr. Carter listened, nodding. There had been a few witnesses, and what Tracy said jibed with what they had reported already. Mr. Carter thanked Tracy, and Tracy returned to his bed and fell asleep immediately.

When he awakened, it was still dark. He might have been asleep only a few hours—others were sleeping in the bunkhouse now—or it might be near dawn and time to start a new day. A twelve-year-old houseboy named Royal was prodding him, whispering that Mr. Carter wanted to see him again.

As he walked toward the big house, the reality of what had happeend at last began to bear down on Tracy. *He's dead! Simon is dead!*

Mr. Carter was in the drawing room, sitting in the chair that made him look like a king. He looked very tired, as tired as Tracy had ever seen him, and his attempt at a friendly smile only emphasized his weariness. Near him sat another man, a much older man, whom Tracy recognized as Mr. Jonas Todd, the lawyer. Mr. Todd, a frequent visitor to the Carter plantation, also smiled at Tracy, and Tracy was instantly wary.

"Sit down, Tracy," Mr. Carter said. "You know Mr. Todd, of course."

Mr. Todd smiled and nodded, and Tracy said, yes, sir, he did know Mr. Todd. He arranged a footstool to sit on. He knew that an invitation to sit down did not mean that he was to take the most comfortable chair that was convenient: he was to sit at his master's feet like a fondly regarded pet.

"First of all," Mr. Carter began, "I want you to know that I appreciate what Simon's death must mean to you. I know how close to him you were, and how fondly he regarded you. I know that the two of you looked on each other very much as father and son might have." *Was he my father?* Tracy asked himself. Perhaps Simon himself had never known for certain.

"I know, too," Mr. Carter said, "that Simon and Hannah shared a great and genuine affection. And never, if I live to the age of Methuselah, will I be able to understand why he turned on her in the manner he did. I can only guess that at the end Simon was utterly mad, and that his death was a blessing to him."

Since an answer was evidently expected of him, Tracy said, "Yes, sir."

"And I want you to know that I share in your grief. Whatever our differences from time to time, Simon was an old and cherished friend. God knows what all I did for that man. Our northern friends can have no idea of what such friendships mean."

"Yes, sir."

"My daughter, as you can imagine, is terribly distraught. For a time this afternoon I actually feared for *her* mental balance. I doubt that we men, Tracy, can fully comprehend the shock that an event like this can deal to the nervous system of a young girl. But the doctor assures me that, in time, Hannah will almost certainly recover and be as good as ever."

"I surely hope so, Mr. Carter."

Mr. Carter nodded. "The main thing, I'm told, is that she must under no circumstances be reminded of the incident. No one must be allowed to say a word to her about it. And she must be removed from the scene of the violence just as quickly as possible. The mind and nerves must be allowed to mend in peace and tranquility."

"I won't say anything to her, Mr. Carter, I promise. And I'll see that nobody else—"

"Thank you, Tracy." Mr. Carter smiled and glanced at Mr. Todd as if everything good he had said about Tracy had been confirmed. "I do trust you, but in any case, there'll be no difficulty on this point. As you've probably heard, I've already arranged for my daughter and her aunt to take a long trip abroad. The doctor tells me that the trip should by no means be delayed, so Hannah and Miz Rachel will be leaving at once."

"Yes, sir."

"I'm telling you about my daughter, Tracy, because you've always been her loyal friend and companion, and you're certainly entitled to know. That brings me to another important matter. I want to express my appreciation of your loyalty. And of your having saved her life."

"I have pointed out," Mr. Todd said in a voice like a rusty hinge, a benign smile still on his face, "that you have done no more than should be expected of a loyal friend and companion."

"Please, Jonas," Mr. Carter said wearily, "we've been all over this. I want to do something for the boy. If he wants to be free, then I want to free him."

The statement came as a shock. But with it came the realization that he *did* want to be free. He had thought about freedom before, but after this last week, he hungered after it as he had never hungered after any other thing in his entire life. With the hunger came the frightening questions, what would he do when he was free? what would happen to him? but the hunger overwhelmed all fears.

"Tracy," Mr. Carter said, "will you accept your freedom?"

"Yes, sir," Tracy said.

"Good. I'm not of the opinion that every black man is fit for freedom, or every white man, for that matter. But I'm sure that a boy of your quality will do well. Now, here is what I propose. I have a second cousin in the state of Ohio. She's an advanced-thinking lady," Mr. Carter said with wry humor, "of abolitionist and utopian views, and I'm sure she'll be delighted to find a home for you in the North. I imagine she'll also be glad to help you continue your education—"

"There are certain practical difficulties," Mr. Todd interrupted.

Tracy suddenly remembered what those difficulties were. "Sir, I ain't—I'm not thirty years old yet. And I just got that—that whipping last week. I don't have four years' good record."

Mr. Todd chuckled. "The boy is well informed. He knows he meets neither qualification for legal manumission in this state—"

"Sir, he saved my daughter's life," Mr. Carter said sharply, and he turned again to Tracy. "There are ways to

60

make the laws bend, boy, if one is discreet. I don't want difficulties with the law or my neighbors, so you must say *nothing* about what we're going to do. As a precaution, you'll stay here in the house for the rest of the night, and you'll leave the plantation tomorrow. As far as everyone else here is concerned, you're simply being transferred to another Carter plantation in another state. This is a reasonable precaution, considering that someone might feel vengeful for your having killed Simon." That was the first time Tracy had heard the fact stated so bluntly, and he flinched.

"Then I'll be freed off the plantation in that other state, sir?"

"Exactly. I think Tennessee would, be best. The law there requires that you be sent out of the state immediately on being freed, but that won't matter, since you'll be going to Ohio. But I must emphasize again the importance of discretion, if we're to arrange this without difficulties. And I think, too, Tracy, that you'd be wise if you stayed out of Tennessee and Louisiana for the rest of your life."

He thought of Hannah. In all likelihood, he would never see her again.

But he would be free.

He said, "I'll be wise, sir."

"And one other thing. You'll need a surname, a family name. Don't feel obliged to do this, but I'd be most pleased if you would take mine."

Tracy Carter.

Tracy Carter liked the sound of it.

PART TWO

chapter one

He knew it wasn't wise to be in Tennessee; he had been warned long ago. But, of course, he was in *Memphis,* Tennessee, and Memphis was a different world. Besides, he was Tracy Carter, that ramblin' white-gloved gamblin' man, black sport and Prince of the River. How was he to go by Memphis and not even get off the boat? No, sir. He had put on his new white hat, and he wore his best white vest under his black coat; he had his knife in his belt and his derringer up his sleeve, and he was loaded for bear.

Memphis was a great town for sport if you knew where to look. There were places where you could bet your money on wrestling men who bucked and kicked like mules and bit and clawed like gators fresh out of the swamps. There were places where fighters stripped to the waist and fought with bare knuckles, circling and pounding for hours like bloody whirlwinds. And there were places, wild places for wild men, where you could eat and drink and the only color that counted was the color of your money, where the women sang songs to scorch your ears and danced dances you couldn't believe. Ah, yes, the women. You paid your money, and you took your choice.

There were the black and the brown and the white. There were the Chinese and the French and the Indian girls, or you could have all three rolled into one. Name your pleasure. The worst of them would cut your throat or rob you blind on a whim. But the best of them!—the best, if they liked you, would teach you delights you had never imagined, joys you could hardly endure.

Tracy was not interested in food or drink or a woman at the moment. Maybe later; not now. His immediate interest was in a tall, muscular, knife-scarred man, half redskin and half black, who wore only a breechclout and who carried a heavy twelve-inch blade honed to an edge that would split a hair or a breastbone with equal ease. Tracy had bet five hundred dollars, even odds, that the half-breed would slash his opponent in three out of five heats. Hamstringing was forbidden. Cutting about the arms, legs, neck, and face was not allowed and did not count. Scratches counted for nothing. The slashes had to be body cuts, solid and clean, and the house's judgment was final.

The fights—cockfights, dogfights, knife fights—took place in a large barnlike structure illuminated by torches; it was filled with a dull smoky glow. The crowd was motley to say the very least. Most of the knife fighters were black, but some were white, a few were of mixed blood, and most were slaves. A number of other blacks were present, some of them free men and gamblers like Tracy, most of them servants to whites. The whites were far in the majority. They included men wearing top hats and men wearing coonskin caps. Planters and traders and riverboat captains—the one thing they had in common was a fistful of money to bet. A number of women joined the crowd—fancy women, whores, mistresses, a few wives, even three or four rich women, here for the forbidden thrill of watching near-naked gladiators fight for blood

The knife fights were conducted in a dozen different ways, hedged about by a hundred sets of rules. Usually there were two fighters, sometimes there might be three or more, confined to a twenty-foot ring down in the pit. Or the ring might be only six feet, and the fighters might have their left wrists or forearms bound together. The fight could go for three out of five cuts, four out of seven, five out of nine. Seldom was it to the death, not only out of fear for the law, but because a fighter was an expensive investment. Still, deaths did occur. Fights in which each participant were given two knives rather than one were particularly dangerous, and there was always the chance that fear or excitement might drive a fighter to murder.

"All bets are covered," a voice said loudly from a cage at the side of the room. "If there's no more bets in one minute, the bank will close!"

The crowd's attention began to focus on the pit, where both fighters stood ready. The half-breed's opponent was a short bull-like black with exceptionally long arms. He wore a pair of faded blue pants, short and tattered, nothing else. His chest was badly scarred, and his face had been slashed several times. He looked grim, while the half-breed looked indifferent. Tracy had seen both men fight before, but he had never seen them fight each other.

"No more bets—" the voice began, and another cut in, "Now, you just wait a minute! I got something to bet, I got something special!" The accent belonged to Mississippi. Tracy tried to see the speaker in the crowd.

"I told you one more minute, sir—"

"You run the bets too fast! You *all* do that when it's even odds! Man can't turn around but you close the betting!"

There were a few murmurs of agreement, and the man came out into the pit looking encouraged. He was a big man dressed in black, his tailoring obviously expensive. He was red-faced and sweating. Tracy thought he recognized him as a local slave trader.

"Now, I got something special!" he repeated.

"What you mean you got something special? You got some money, you put it up, and I'll keep the bank open another minute. Anybody want to wager against this gentleman?"

"You bet they do, they all do, they all here for Johnny Cheer!" The man chanted like an auctioneer, and Tracy knew that he was indeed a slaver. "They all going to bet again' my prize—"

"How much, sir?"

"Just a minute, you going to *see* how much!"

Johnny Cheer darted away from the pit, as a rustle of impatience went through the crowd. But he immediately reappeared, leading a young black woman by the arm. At a glance, there was nothing particularly unusual about her. She was simply a female, small but pretty. Her hair grew high and uncut. She had gold rings in her ears, a gold necklace around her throat, and on her arms and one ankle, she had several bracelets of silver; yet she wore an ordinary white cotton dress and sandals.

Then Cheer brought her closer to Tracy, and he saw that she was beautiful. There was a line of eye and lip, a delicacy of cheek and jawbone, such as he had never seen before.

The crowd groaned; they were looking for cash, a bet, and a fight, and if Johnny Cheer wanted to bet, he should have brought money, not a woman.

"Sir," came the voice of the banker, "this is a sporting establishment, but not a cathouse. Neither do we conduct slave auctions—"

"I ain't auctioning nobody! I am *betting* this here piece of class-A, hardly-been-touched, fancy goods on the black boy against the half-breed. And what I want to know *now* is how much one of you gentlemen is willing to wager against this beautiful young black damsel!"

"Sir, you cannot do that—"

"Don't you worry, Mr. Banker, you going to get your percentage!"

More groans, and demands that Johnny Cheer be thrown out. Tracy tried unsuccessfully to catch the black girl's eye. She looked into the distance, her eyes blank, and her face expressionless. If she felt humiliated, she was careful to give no sign.

"I am closing this bank."

"Now, wait a minute—"

"Two dollars against the bitch," someone said, laughing.

"Make it three!"

"I'll bid four."

"Four and a quarter?"

"One thousand dollars," Tracy said. He said it flatly

and calmly but loud enough to be heard, and the tone of the murmuring within the crowd immediately changed.

Cheer looked delighted. "Now, that's what I like to hear! This gentleman is willing to bet one thousand dollars on the half-breed against this lovely female, and he hasn't even seen the best of her yet!"

With that, he gripped the back of the girl's dress at the neck. His fists tightened and pulled apart, and the cotton ripped. The dress fell to the ground, and the girl stood naked before the crowd.

Naked, that is, except for the earrings, the necklace, and the bracelets, with all their calculated effect. The girl seemed to be unaware of her nakedness, or too proud to hide the nipples on the high firm breasts or the dark arrowhead on the pubic mound. Every eye was on her now, and every eye saw, as well as Tracy did, her perfection.

"This bank is closed!" came the angry call.

"Well, you can just open it up again," someone said. "I'll bet twelve hundred against the girl."

"Fifteen hundred," Tracy said.

"Sixteen," said someone else.

"Gentlemen," Johnny Cheer said, "you ain't really looked at this wench yet. Walk around for 'em, Alexandria—let 'em all see! She comes with two full bags of fancy clothes! She was a rich man's darling since childhood, and like I said, she ain't hardly been touched! But she knows what to do, or he wouldn't never have kept her!"

The girl walked around the pit as gracefully as if she had been alone. Only the two fighters refused to look at her, keeping their eyes to the ground. Johnny Cheer's stratagem was obvious, but nonetheless effective. The girl would have brought a thousand dollars or perhaps twelve hundred on the current market. He was hoping to bid a thousand dollars against a great deal more—at even odds. But the crowd, now enjoying itself, either forgot this fact or chose to ignore it.

"Seventeen hundred," someone yelled.

"Eighteen."

"Two thousand," Tracy said, and finally the girl looked at him.

"Two thousand," Johnny Cheer said. "The black gentleman will bet two thousand dollars on the half-breed. Against this here beautiful prime wench. And her not even eighteen years old yet! One of you gentlemen can top two thousand dollars!"

Tracy tried to guess the girl's age; he thought she must be in her early twenties, no matter what Johnny Cheer might say. Her eyes had lost their blank look now: they were curious, speculative; intelligent brown eyes that tried to see into him, tried to read him. But there was still not the slightest sign that she was made self-conscious by the eyes that were on her.

No one was offering to top two thousand dollars.

"No one else?" Johnny Cheer asked. "For another hundred dollars you can have the opportunity—"

"Sir," came the bored voice from the bank, "we cannot prolong this all night—"

"Twenty-one hundred," said Ethan Flynn.

Tracy had not seen Ethan until the very instant that he spoke. He heard the voice, recognized it, and saw the man. Ethan was standing directly across the pit, and he was flanked by two knife-scarred blacks, one a giant and the other a bantam. Even after eleven years, the placid good-natured face, the slow smile, the lazy but frosty eyes were all exactly as Tracy remembered them.

Eleven years . . .

He seldom looked back past those eleven years, but he looked back now. He remembered being bathed in sweat and blood, his body lacerated. He remembered the terror as he was thrown onto his back and his knees were forced to his shoulders. He remembered the youth with the good-natured face and the lazy smile who had grasped his genitals and brought a knife blade against them.

"I don't hardly know where to begin."

Tracy had much to remember Ethan for. He had terrorized Tracy and made him appear less a man in Hannah's eyes. If not for him, Tracy and Hannah would never have been whipped, and Hannah and her aunt might never have been sent abroad. Simon would never have had his drunken murderous rage, and Tracy would never have killed Simon.

And, ironically, Tracy would not have been a free man today.

But his freedom did not redeem the evil. Nothing could do that. There had been times of self-doubt, times when Tracy had blamed himself for all the bad that had happened. But not now; not as a man. Now he traced it all back to Ethan—Ethan, who stood across the pit from him and smiled and shrugged as if to apologize for his twenty-one hundred.

"Twenty-five hundred," Tracy said, wondering if Ethan recognized him. It didn't seem likely.

"Now, you know you don't want to gamble twenty-five hundred against that little gal, boy," Ethan said. "She ain't worth it. She ain't worth twenty-one hundred, for that matter, but I'm a charitable man, and her master he looks hungry."

There was a ripple of laughter, but the voice of the banker was heard once again: "Gentlemen, we cannot wait any longer—"

Ethan spoke toward the banker's cage: *"Now, you just hold it, boy— we are arranging a bet!"* His voice for an instant was harsh and snarling mean, belying the good-natured face. The room became completely silent. The girl —Alexandria—and the two fighters appeared frozen. Ethan Flynn was used to having things his own way.

"We were saying," Ethan began again smoothly.

"I was saying twenty-five hundred. I still am."

"You're still a fool, Stacy, boy. I nearly took your balls off once, and now I'm gon' do it for sure."

So Ethan recognized him. Tracy was pleased that he did. "The name is Tracy Carter, and you're welcome to try."

Ethan blinked, and for an instant his smile vanished. "Carter, huh?" He looked away from Tracy and toward Alexandria's master. "Mr. Cheer—if that's your name—"

"Johnny Cheer, sir—Cheer is here! Make it three thousand—"

"I'll do nothing of the sort. Mr. Cheer, that nigger over

there is willing to bet twenty-five hundred. *I* am willing to match that. *I* am willing to place twenty-five hundred against that wench of yours, and I expect you to accept *my* money."

This development was clearly a surprise to Cheer—as it was to Tracy. He looked nervously at Tracy and back at Ethan, flanked by his giant and his bantam.

"Sir, the black gentleman placed his bet first—"

"I don't give a damn when he placed it, Mr. Cheer. I say a white man's bet takes precedence over that of a nigger. You're going to take my bet, Mr. Cheer, and you damn well better believe it."

"If you would place a somewhat higher bet—"

"No. Mr. Carter over there can place a higher bet if he wishes, and maybe I'll meet it and maybe I won't, but if I *do* meet it, you're going to take *my* money. Now, isn't that right?"

Johnny Cheer looked at Tracy again, perhaps hoping that Tracy would raise his proposed bet. But Tracy knew there was no point in doing so. His funds were not unlimited, and Ethan could buy and sell him a thousand times over. He could force Ethan to go higher, but that would only amuse the white man. Moreover, Ethan might dump Tracy at any time, perhaps at a dangerously high level, and then if Tracy lost . . . the humiliation of being stripped by Ethan would be even worse than the loss of fifteen or twenty thousand dollars.

Tracy was sick with impotent fury.

He shook his head.

"You don't want to raise your bet?" Cheer asked.

"No."

"You're withdrawing your bet?"

"No, goddammit, I'm not withdrawing my bet! I offered a bet of twenty-five hundred dollars, and I haven't heard anybody top it! It's *my bet!*"

"I'm sorry, but you know a white gentleman has got to get first chance. . . ."

Across the pit, Ethan chuckled. He held out his right hand, palm up and cupped, and shook it as if he were rattling something.

Tracy's balls.

Under any other circumstances, Tracy would have found the fight interesting. The participants sparred for several minutes, exploring each other's style and collecting a few insignificant scratches. The half-breed then made a good try for a belly cut, but collected a chest wound instead. A moment later, the black gave him a second chest wound. Then the half-breed first cut the black across the ribs. After considerable sparring, he managed to inflict a second cut on the ribs, and then, almost instantly, he dealt a slash across the belly, winning the fight. In the final heat, the black had also managed to inflict a belly wound, and Cheer tried to insist that he had struck first. He was clearly wrong and was overruled. Ethan Flynn paid the house percentage and collected the girl. Tracy had found little point in hoping that Ethan would lose, and he found little consolation in the five hundred dollars he himself had won.

"Let me buy a drink," Ethan said, smiling, as they stood by the banker's cage.

Tracy returned the smile bleakly. "Drink with the man who's been after my balls all these years?" Ethan Flynn was the last man in the world he wanted to drink with.

Ethan laughed and slapped Tracy's shoulder. "Don't take it so seriously. You seem to be all in one piece. I just thought you'd like to know how things are back home. Come on, now, I got a thirst."

Tracy followed Ethan and his entourage into an adjoining room where the bar and the tables were planks on barrel heads and where sawdust covered the floor. The smell of barbecued meat was thick in the smoky air. The girl had pulled a fresh dress from one of her overstuffed bags and had put it on. Tracy wanted to catch her eye again, but her face was as expressionless as before, and she kept it averted from him.

Ethan made the girl sit beside him at one of the plank tables, and Tracy sat facing the pair. A bottle and glasses were put between them. The other two blacks, the giant and the bantam, stood nearby. Black and white could eat, drink, gamble, and even wench together here, because this was not a respectable place. It existed in a man's world, and the very fact that women were here, whores and wives alike, showed what it was. In a truly respectable tavern, women would not have been permitted near the bar. The very banning of women was a testament of respectability.

But even here, ultimately, the white man's word was law. Tracy had just received a stinging reminder of that fact.

"Back home," he prompted after Ethan had poured whiskey. In the other room, there was a barking and howling; a dogfight was about to begin.

"What do you want to know?"

Tracy hesitated, afraid to say what he truly wanted to know. Instead, he said, "Mr. Carter."

"Dead. Long dead. Died about a year after I married Hannah."

So Ethan had married Hannah despite all; he said so with no special emphasis, looking straight at Tracy.

And, Hannah had married Ethan.

Well, why not? He had been the most eligible young man available. He was rich, handsome, high-spirited, intelligent, a womanizer—all the things a young white man was supposed to be back home. He and Hannah had been marked for each other since childhood.

And yet, Tracy felt somehow betrayed.

"You're a fortunate man, Mr. Ethan," he said. "Miss Hannah was a fine young lady."

"Oh, she still is, Tracy," Ethan said, with a faint mocking tone in his voice. "She still is."

"And Miz Rachel?"

"Dead, too. In Europe. Hannah come home when Miz Rachel died. They're all dead now, Tracy, all the ole folk. Hannah's, mine . . ."

They sat quietly for a moment, as if feeling their own mortality.

"I take it you're traveling," Tracy said. "Is your wife traveling with you?"

Ethan laughed and looked at the girl, Alexandria. He put his hand on the girl's thigh under the table, and her lower lip curled disdainfully for an instant, but she showed no further expression.

"Hannah don't do much traveling," Ethan said, still looking at the girl and moving his hand. "She goes to town now and then, that's about all. Me, I travel a lot. I got seven plantations to look after now, you know, not to speak of all the tenant farms and other businesses, and I try to get to each plantation at least once every year or two." He turned away from the girl and poured more whiskey. "Now you see why I pick me up a little traveling companion now and then. I figure on heading back downriver to New Orleans in a day or so, and this little gal ought to keep me pleasured till I get there, don't you think?"

So that's the way it is, Tracy thought.

The pattern was a familiar one; he realized that it was far more common than he had suspected as a boy. A white man married, but refused to give up his black wenches. The wife, embittered, then turned cold if she were not already, or turned promiscuous, or turned to some vicious combination of the two. The man took this as an excuse to continue his wenching. His son grew up to emulate his behavior, and his daughter emulated the behavior of her mother; the cycle was self-perpetuating from generation to generation.

How would it have affected Hannah? He had no idea of how she would have reacted to it. He had been away from her for far too many years—for more than a third of his lifetime. But remembering Hannah, remembering how beautiful she had been as a girl, how high-spirited and lusty and fun-loving, he could only look at the man who had married her and think, *What a waste. . . .*

"What about you?" Ethan asked. "What you doing here? Last place I'd ever expect to see a Carter nigger."

"I'm not a Carter nigger," Tracy said carefully.

"Oh, I know. I sorta wondered what happened to you. I seen long ago in our Tennessee records that ole Addison set you free. That why you took his name? out of gratitude?"

"Call it a souvenir of Hannah."

Ethan gave him a sharp look. *"Miz* Hannah?"

"Mrs. Flynn."

Ethan laughed. "You're a real uppity nigger for one that nearly lost his balls! I like that!" But Tracy knew he did not.

"You're a gambling man, huh?" Ethan said after a minute.

"I've been known to make a wager."

The white man shook his head meditatively. "Up here they don't know how to fight with knives the way they do in Louisiana. Knife fighting and stick fighting, you see the best in New Orleans. I done some of it myself, got me some cuts. Ever done any knife fighting, boy?"

"No."

"I hold fights in my barn, you know, down in Louisiana. Got me some good boys. Give 'em some time off from the fields and some whiskey and a good-looking wench to fight for, and they'll cut each other up all day and all night." Ethan looked at Alexandria. "How'd you like to take on a ole cut-up bull of a knife fighter? Maybe you get a chance when I get you down home. . . . I asked you a question, honey."

The girl shrugged. She looked at Tracy, and for some reason, he was not sure why, he felt ashamed. Perhaps it was just that he was sitting with a knife in his belt and a gun up his sleeve and he was doing nothing about this grinning, pink-faced bastard.

"Gambling man," Ethan said, "I want to book passage for New Orleans on a boat where a man can make an honest wager. Which one do I take?"

"Mine."

He had not meant to say it. He had meant to leave this place and never see Ethan Flynn again. But he was not ready to part from Ethan yet.

"You're *that* Tracy Carter," Ethan said, grinning. "I sort of wondered."

"The *Duchess of Cairo* leaves for New Orleans tomorrow. Some of the best cabins are still available. I run the gambling lounge, and I run it honest. It never closes as long as you're there to make a bet. It's open right now, as a matter of fact, and you may go aboard at any time."

"Yes, I been thinking I'd try the *Duchess of Cairo*. I guess you and me were bound to run into each other sooner or later, Tracy, boy."

"When do you want to board her?"

"You said the gambling lounge was open—suppose you show us the way to your boat."

They stood up from the table. Ethan paid the bill. The

giant and the bantam picked up the two bags, and Tracy led the way out.

He had no idea what he was going to do about Ethan; it was unlikely that he would be able to do anything at all. But he was a professional gambler, and Ethan Flynn was not, and Ethan was about to enter Tracy's territory. They would be together on the boat for several days and nights, and in that time, something, some opportunity to best Ethan, might develop. At any rate, Tracy could hope.

chapter two

Lights burned brightly on the *Duchess of Cairo* as they boarded her, and music could be heard from one of the lounges. Ethan's servants carried most of the luggage, and a dockhand carried the rest. A steward led the way to the cabin Ethan had booked for himself and Alexandria. The giant and the midget would travel as deck passengers.

"Sounds lively," Ethan remarked as they walked closer to the music.

"It's always lively on the *Duchess,*" Tracy said.

"Is the food good?"

"Excellent."

"And the service?"

"Terrible."

Ethan laughed. River steamers were not noted for the excellence of their service, as both he and Tracy knew well. Tracy was giving him a chance to be pleasantly surprised.

They parted at the door to Ethan's cabin.

"I'll be in the gambling lounge in a half-hour or so," Ethan said. "No danger of their closing the door on me?"

"No danger. We'll be busy for hours yet."

"Then I'll see you there."

"You'll see me."

The door closed, and Tracy stood in the darkness. Not that it was very dark—light poured out of the windows of those cabins that were already occupied and from a hundred points around the docks. A steamboat was like a hotel, and it tried to fill its rooms as completely and as early as it could: it had bars, dining rooms, a barbershop, a gambling lounge, all of which had overhead and could only make a profit when there were customers aboard. Tracy had known there would be a cabin available for Ethan because, like many a crowded hotel, the *Duchess* kept space in reserve for a few special guests.

Tracy wandered about the boat. He went into the gambling lounge, asked his assistant if there were any problems, found that all was going smoothly. His men were honest and well trained. He went into the bar off the lounge and chatted with the black bartender. The dining room was in operation, and he stopped in the kitchen for a cup of hot, black, Deep South coffee. He looked into the dining room and the main lounge to see if there were any interesting looking passengers, passengers who might like to try their luck at a game. Sometimes the interesting passengers were women who were traveling alone. A surprising number of them preferred sharing spacious quarters with a handsome black gambler to traveling alone in a cramped cabin. And who was he not to accommodate these lovely ladies?

But he saw no possibilities this evening, and he went up to the pilot house, where Captain Standish was conferring with his engineer. The three men chatted amiably for a few minutes, and Tracy went out on deck again to look at the hundred lights and to sniff the spicy atmosphere of the docks.

This was home. It had been home since this particular steamer was built several years ago. This one was his baby, though he was responsible for the gambling operation on six others as well. He had his own cabin, one of the best on the boat. He ordered anything he wished from the menu and never paid. And he received a share of the house percentage on every one of his seven steamers, giving him a steady, healthy income. He owned shares in the company, and he planned to buy more. If he played his cards right, he might one day be a very wealthy man.

Yes, this was his home. This was his life, the life he had made for himself, and he had no intention of changing it. But he had come a long, long way to get here. . . .

His stay with Miss Fayette Williams began on a note of farce and, in some respects, stayed on that note as long as he was with her.

On Mr. Carter's orders, he was given a full bag of fine new clothes fit for northern winters, five dollars spending money, and a steamer ticket to Cincinnati. The five dollars was deemed more than sufficient, since he wasn't expected to eat in the dining room from the white folks' bill of fare. The assistant overseer of the Tennessee plantation saw him aboard at Memphis, and he traveled up the Mississippi to Cairo and up the Ohio to his destination. Meanwhile, he ran into some boys rolling bones just the way they did back home, and he parlayed his five dollars into two hundred fifty.

At Cincinnati, he was met by an elderly friend of Miss Williams.

"*You're* Tracy Carter?" he said. "*You're* Tracy Carter?"

"Yes, sir," Tracy said, and the man shook his head with amazement and disapproval. Tracy figured Miss Williams had forgot to warn him that Tracy was black.

But after the man had driven Tracy all the way to the little town where Miss Fayette Williams lived, and after Tracy had got out of the buggy and lugged his bag all the way to the door, and after Miss Fayette Williams had opened the door and looked out, he realized that *that* wasn't the problem at all.

Miss Williams gazed at him in horror and said, "But you're a *boy!*"

It seemed that, on the evidence of Tracy's name, Miss Williams had been expecting a girl. She had quite overlooked anything in Addison Carter's letters that had stated the contrary. Later Tracy was to suspect that she had *wanted* to overlook anything that had stated the contrary.

She recovered from her initial shock at once. She decid-

80

ed that since he *was* only a boy, and since she was a lady of advanced views, there was certainly nothing wrong with taking him into her home. And he was a refugee from *slavery,* poor child! How could she live with herself if she betrayed her ideals the first time they were put to the test? She had a beautiful little room waiting for Tracy up under the eaves.

Tracy liked Miss Fayette, as he came to call her, he liked her very much. She was about twice his age. She had an attractive figure, more or less, and her face had a slightly *scrunched-down* quality like a monkey or a bulldog. He would not have said that Miss Fayette was ugly—he had been attracted to girls who were uglier—but he sensed that she was of a different opinion.

Tracy did the yard work and ran errands and generally did whatever he could to make himself useful. He met various townspeople, but he could not honestly say that he made friends. He discovered that, as the only black boy living in town, he was regarded as something of a freak. There were plenty of blacks around this part of the country, but not in town. Not in *this* town, by George! Who does Fayette Williams think she is, keeping nigger help in town and living in her own house?

"She's a saint! She's a saint!" many of the women said. "But the trouble is, she's crazy!"

The feeling that he was a freak became even worse after school started. Other black children, if they went to school at all, went to a little one-room building in the country, and few continued their schooling for long. It was Miss Fayette's opinion that Tracy already knew more than the teacher of *that* school, so she insisted that he be enrolled in town.

As it turned out, he was accepted readily enough. The fact that most of the children in his room were younger than him did not particularly bother him—there were a number of over-age louts as well. He was bothered by having to sit in a back corner of the room. Now, he knew perfectly well that *some*body had to sit in that back corner. But why did they have to make him feel that that back corner was a special place, just for him?

He did well. In fact, he did much better than anyone

else in the room. This little fact got him smacked in the nose by one of the louts during a lunch period. The incident happened in the schoolyard, and when he tried to fight back, he was immediately grabbed by half a dozen kids, and the cry went up, "The nigger's gone crazy!" "He's turned into a savage again!" "He's a goddam cannibal—he bit George!"

The teacher made him stay after school for two weeks as a punishment, and she very gently explained to him why. The punishment, she said, was simply to help him remember some very important facts. He was never to forget that he was a Negro. It was most important that he set an example for others. He must be modest and unassuming, kind and sweet-natured. He must exercise whatever intelligence he might have to the very limit, but he must never preen himself on his cleverness. And he must always be ready to demonstrate to one and all that he, Tracy Carter, was a credit to his race.

It was a white lady speaking, so Tracy managed to hold his tongue. But he did wonder why the white kids couldn't try setting an example for *him* and being a credit to *their* race. Somehow that never seemed to enter white folks' minds.

Meanwhile, Miss Fayette contributed to Tracy's education by informing him of her advanced views. Fortunately she had an independent income from tenant farms, for these views had caused her to lose her job as a schoolteacher. Once considered a threat to the morals of the young, she was now thought of as a harmless eccentric.

It seemed that Miss Fayette was an enthusiast of farm colonies and communal living, and this was what Addison Carter had meant when he had referred to her utopian views. She knew all about the Ephrata community in Pennsylvania and the Amana society in Iowa. She explained the views of Robert Owen and Charles Fourier to Tracy, and she lectured to him on New Harmony and Brook Farm. She had exchanged letters with Ralph Waldo Emerson and Nathaniel Hawthorne, and she carried on a lively correspondence with half a dozen other utopian leaders.

"It's the wave of the future," she told Tracy. "These

various advanced communities do differ from each other, of course, and some are religious and others secular, but the pattern is becoming clear. In our day, we shall see the time when virtually *all* citizens shall live in such communities. Black and white shall live together. Women shall have the vote, and they shall no longer be confined to the home. They shall toil in the fields shoulder to shoulder with the men—"

"You mean you really *want* to toil in the fields, Miss Fayette?" Tracy had never yet met a female field hand who *wanted* to be one.

"Why, yes! Of course! That's equality! And womankind will no longer be man's chattel. Her body shall be her own. We shall no longer own each other's bodies and souls. I am for the abolition of slavery for white women as much as for black people, Tracy. A woman shall be free to choose the father of her child—and a different father for each child, if she so desires. I am a great advocate of selective breeding. Do I shock you?"

Tracy was a little surprised but not shocked. While families were kept more or less intact on the Carter plantation in Louisiana, he knew of others where they were not, and he knew of many black women who had whelped babies with different fathers. This selective breeding business was, in his view, not an unmixed blessing. Somehow, despite her extensive knowledge and intricate theories, Miss Fayette struck Tracy as being rather an innocent, and because of that, he liked her all the more.

"Babies should be brought up in nurseries," she lectured. "All should be brothers and sisters to each other. All women should be their mothers, and all men should be their fathers. All should love one another like one big happy family—"

"Miss Fayette," he interrupted one day, "you talk about these places all the time—why don't you go join one?"

Surprisingly, she blushed. "Oh, no. I'm too old . . . and set in my ways. . . ."

She meant that she was afraid of being disillusioned on the one hand and rejected on the other. He learned that she had not always held these advanced views. Shy and puritanical, she had decided at the age of twenty-five that

she was doomed to be an old maid; then, in a kind of rebellion, she had turned to utopianism. But all she could do
now was write her letters and preach her gospel to Tracy,
growing pink in the face as she talked of "selective breeding" and "giving each of one's children a different father"
and everybody being "one big happy family."

Sometimes she did startle Tracy. "Are you a virgin?"
she asked one day. "Don't be afraid to tell me. I've heard
that slaves lead *terribly* promiscuous sexual lives, but you
know that I believe the bonds of love should be unshackled and youth allowed to explore and learn. *Are* you a virgin?"

Tracy was not at all sure what answer was expected
from him, what he could safely say.

"Well, I don't know exactly," he said at last.

"You don't know! Either you are or you aren't, aren't
you?"

"Well, I don't know. I played, you know, like most
kids, we played, little boys and girls, then maybe not so
little—" he was more embarrassed than he would have expected—"but at what point exactly does a boy stop being
a virgin? Or when does a girl, if you look at the matter just
right? I mean, just exactly at *wha-a-a-at point* do you
stop?"

Miss Fayette blushed. "Why, I had never thought of it
that way!"

When he was at home with Miss Fayette, he could forget all about the louts of the school yard and the patroniz-
ing or discriminating whites of the town. He stopped feeling so much like a freak when he was with her. If he *was* a
freak, well, then they were freaks together. He knew she
genuinely liked him, and he liked her.

But all was not well, even at home. There was a snake
in the Garden of Eden.

The problem first manifested itself about a month after
Tracy's arrival. Two or three times a week Miss Fayette
had an eighteen-year-old girl named Ona in to help her
with her housework. She and Tracy had little to do with
one another, but he tried to behave pleasantly toward her.
And one afternoon, to his surprise, Miss Fayette called

him into the sitting room and addressed him with a sharp tongue and bleak eyes.

"Tracy, I want you to know that *I* know what's been going on, and I am deeply disappointed in you."

"Ma'am?"

"Oh, don't you try to look innocent. I've heard you and Ona giggling in the kitchen—"

"Ma'am?"

"—and I do not approve, Tracy, I most certainly do not approve. . . ."

Forgotten was her contention that "the bonds of love should be unshackled and youth allowed to explore and learn." At that first incident, Tracy hardly dared protest his innocence; but he learned to do so.

"Tracy, you promised me that you would not lead Ona on—"

"Miss Fayette, I thought you finally understood that nothing's going on between Ona and me—"

"I am not blind, Tracy! Now, you're going to give me no choice but to let that girl go—"

"But Miss Fayette—"

"I will not have it said that *I* was responsible for that girl having a black baby—"

"I don't see how you *could* be!"

"I think we had best have this out once and for all. . . ."

But they "had it out" time and again, usually at intervals of less than two weeks and sometimes less than twenty-four hours. And Ona was not the only female of whom Miss Fayette was jealous. There was Tracy's schoolteacher. There was a teenage girl who lived down the street. There was Miss Fayette's best friend, a widow who sometimes "borrowed" Tracy to help her with her yardwork. And the list of possibilities yet to be explored was almost endless.

Tracy knew exactly why Miss Fayette acted as she did; he had had long acquaintance with bitchy females back on the plantation. And Miss Fayette herself sometimes showed surprising insight into her motivations: "I'm sorry, Tracy, I know I've been acting like a jealous old maid, and I suppose that's exactly what I am. . . ." But her insight and Tracy's understanding and diplomacy were not enough to halt the increasing frequency and vehemence of their arguments; and one cold sleety morning in early February, he decided he had had quite enough.

"I'm sorry, Miss Fayette, but I've got to leave here. I can't take this anymore. I don't want you to think I'm an ungrateful boy after all you've done for me, but—"

"You can't leave!" she said, shocked. "Why, you're just a—a child—"

"A child! I'm eighteen! Lots of boys eighteen have been earning their way for years."

Now she was truly shocked. "Eighteen? You're eighteen? When did you turn eighteen? You didn't even tell me!"

"Sometime early this month. I'm not just sure."

"But eighteen is a *man!*"

"That's what I'm saying. And I think I'd better leave here—"

"We'll talk about it this evening."

But they did not talk about it that evening. When he arrived home from school, her mood was as cheerful as it had ever been since he had come to live with her. After he had done his chores and cleaned up, he found that she had cooked him a beautiful ham-and-yam birthday dinner, complete with a huge candle-bedecked cake. They ate and talked and laughed together, ate still more until they were stuffed, laughed until they were falling apart, and not a word was said about their quarrels. They spent half the evening at the table, and when at last they stood up, Miss Fayette said, "Now that you're a man, you're too old for a birthday spanking, but at least I can give you a birthday kiss."

She walked to him, and he lowered his head, expecting a peck on the forehead or the cheek. That was not what he got. Her head tilted to one side, and her hands went to his waist. Her lips pressed against his. Startled, he almost pulled his face away, but their mouths remained together. Her hands slid over his back, and her arms tightened around him as she pressed the full length of her body against his. He felt as paralyzed as a fly being eaten by a spider, unable either to respond or to break away.

And the kiss went on and on and on. . . .

Miss Fayette ended it. With a little sob, she tore herself away from him and ran up the stairs that led to her bedroom.

Tracy at once set about the task of cleaning up the dining room and washing the dishes. Even though he was now alone, he struggled to keep from grinning in too broad and boyish a fashion: a really and truly grown up woman, twice as old as he, had kissed him like a *man!* For the moment, at least, that seemed to make all of Miss Fayette's bitchiness worthwhile.

When the dining room and the kitchen were tidied up, he spent an hour or so studying his lessons, and he managed to put Miss Fayette out of his mind. Then he made a fast trip to the cold privy out back, returned and washed himself up in the kitchen, and went up the stairs toward his attic bedroom.

The crack under Miss Fayette's door made a thin line of light.

His bedroom was cold. He undressed as quickly as he could and slipped shivering between the frigid sheets and under the thick comforters. He reached toward the lamp to put it out. He had just touched it when he heard the tapping at the door, and he drew quickly back into bed.

"Come in."

Miss Fayette was bundled up in at least two nightgowns, a robe, a scarf, fur slippers, and a sleeping cap. "I heard you come upstairs," she said. "I just thought I'd see if everything was all right."

"Oh, yes, ma'am. Everything's all right."

"Are you sure there's nothing I can do for you?"

"No, ma'am. I'm fine."

"It's terribly cold tonight. Are you sure you don't need more blankets——"

"Oh, no, ma'am. I'm warm as toast."

"Well . . . all right."

She stood by the doorway as if reluctant to leave. After a few seconds, she hurried to his bedside and sat down on a chair, drawing it closer to him.

"Tracy, I do feel that we should talk for a few minutes."

"All right, ma'am."

She frowned. "Your shoulders are bare! Don't you have your night clothes on?"

"Like you've got? Miss Fayette, I never had anything like that in my life."

"I wish I'd known. I'll have to make you some. Are you sure you're not—"

"No, no, really, I *like* sleeping like this. But what did you want to talk about?"

Miss Fayette swallowed hard, and as nearly as he could tell in the lamp light, she was blushing. "First, I want to apologize for kissing you the way I did. And for running off. You see, I was very embarrassed. I had meant the kiss to be totally innocent, but I had forgotten to take into account the fact that you are now a grown man. And I am a woman."

"But you don't have to apologize for kissing me, ma'am. We're friends, ain't we—aren't we?"

"Yes, but—"

"I'm *glad* you kissed me."

"You are?"

"I'm just sorry I didn't kiss you back better than I did."

Miss Fayette managed a smile. "Well, I know I am not an attractive woman—"

"Now, why do you want to say that! I think you must spend half your life telling yourself you're not attractive and nobody wants you, and that's plain silly!"

"But I'm not at all—"

"Miss Fayette, you're a very attractive lady! Listen, I've known some really *ugly* ladies who were attractive, but you—you're sort of pretty, in your own way, and you've got a nice enough shape, and you can cook and sew like nobody I ever knew before—"

"Then why has no man ever wanted me, Tracy? You can tell me quite frankly. Remember, I am a liberated woman."

"I'm not saying no man ever has. But if that's true . . . do you really want me to tell you what I think?"

She nodded. "I am not frightened by the brute facts of life."

"Well, Miss Fayette, haven't you spent an awful lot of time persuading men that you don't want *them?*"

"Why, no!" Miss Fayette looked shocked.

"You told me that before you were twenty-five you were—what was that word?—very puritanical. And after twenty-five, you scandalized everybody with your advanced ideas. Sounds to me like you've been working pretty hard to keep the men folk away."

She stared down at his face, and he pulled his arms out from under the covers and put his hands behind his head. He felt very much in command of the situation.

"Do you mean you think I've been running away from men?" she asked.

"You sure ran up those stairs this evening."

"But that was altogether different! You didn't want my kiss—"

"Miss Fayette, lean down here."

Hesitantly, as if she had some idea of what he intended but was not quite sure, she leaned forward. He reached up with one arm and pulled her head down the rest of the way. Their lips met, and this time he kissed her—lightly, gently, tenderly. He felt very proud of himself, very *free*.

He released her. "What did you mean," he asked, "I didn't want your kiss?"

"Oh, Tracy!" She slowly lifted her head. She looked groggy and seemed to be gasping for air. "You make me feel like such a child. I talk about being liberated, but you know so much more than I do, and you've had so much more experience! Tracy, would you kiss me again?"

He sat up in bed, and the covers fell to his lap. For an instant, Miss Fayette looked vaguely frightened, but when Tracy reached for her, she moved from her chair to the side of the bed and into the circle of Tracy's arm. He ignored the cold. With a true instinct for power, he knew that in some way he had the upper hand over Miss Fayette. She looked like a child bundled up in her nightclothes, she felt like a child in his arms, and he kissed her like a child. Paradoxically, even the fact of her much greater age made her seem in some way childlike.

"Tracy," she said after a moment, her voice a tremulous whisper, "I'm just a virginal old maid."

"Don't talk like that."

"It's true." Her hand moved over his chest. "But you—

you've had experience. You're not afraid of the—the female sex, are you? I mean, you don't run away."

"Of course not."

"And you *do* like me?"

"You must know I do!"

"And you don't find me repulsive?"

"Miss Fayette, I keep telling you—"

"Oh, Tracy, darling, I don't want to die a virgin!"

In the next instant, her mouth was again covering his, while her hand shot down to grab at him under the covers.

And he panicked.

This was not *at all* what he had had in mind! Somewhere along the way there had been a terrible misunderstanding! His sense of power, his sense of command of the situation, vanished utterly, and he floundered. He tried to remove his mouth from Miss Fayette's and failed: he felt as if he were suffocating. He flailed about and kicked at the covers. If Miss Fayette didn't let go of him, she would certainly injure him permanently! Her hand unmanned him as effectively as Ethan Flynn's had and without even threatening him with a knife.

As abruptly as she had seized him, Miss Fayette gave up the struggle. She twisted away, hiding her face. "Oh, what am I doing!" she wailed. "You don't want me! I'm just an ugly old woman, trying to seduce a young man, and I'm so ashamed!"

And for the second time that evening, she fled from him.

Tracy sank back onto his bed and waited for the thumping of his heart to slow and his panic to die. After a moment, he drew the sheet and comforters back over himself, though he hardly noticed the cold.

He had been scared silly. He had to admit that to himself. And the terror had had absolutely nothing to do with Ethan Flynn's knife or Addison Carter's whipping post or the fact that every white man he had ever known had wanted him to stand in awe of white women. The terror had proceeded from the fact that he was an eighteen-year-old boy who was not used to having an older woman attack him sexually—and clumsily at that.

Poor Miss Fayette, he thought. Once the panic was

gone, he began to feel sick at the thought of Miss Fayette's humiliation. Now she would be too mortified to look him in the face, and he would be too embarrassed to remain here with her. He would have to carry out his determination to leave the house, and the sooner the better. And it was all so unnecessary. If only he hadn't been so childish, if only he had responded more like an experienced adult . . .

Because after all, he thought, it wasn't as if he didn't like Miss Fayette. He liked her very much. And he was telling her the plain truth when he said she was much more attractive than she believed. Right at the present moment she seemed very attractive. . . .

And if he hadn't lost his head, if he had behaved more as a man would have behaved, she would still be with him . . .

What an opportunity he had lost! Why, she had actually been begging him to give her a pleasuring! It was the very kind of situation a growing boy dreamed about! By this time, he should have had her in bed with him. . . .

He groaned.

Now that it was too late, he needed her as much as she had needed him. He hadn't been this wrought up in months, not since that last time he went swimming with Hannah. Still, look at how *that* had ended; he had best forget all about Miss Fayette and go to sleep.

He could not. He put out the light and lay back, but five minutes later he was as awake and as miserable as ever.

With another groan, he threw back the covers and sat up on the edge of the bed. There was only one way that he knew to resolve this situation. He felt his way through the dark to the door. He did not bother to dress, cold though it was. He went out onto the landing and down the dark stairs; he followed the second-floor hallway to Miss Fayette's room. The thin line of light still showed along the doorjamb, and Tracy heard muffled sobs.

He tapped lightly on the door, but there was no answer. He tapped again, a little harder. When there was still no answer, only the constant sobbing, he opened the door and walked into the room.

He gaped with astonishment.

The two nightgowns, the robe, the scarf, the fur slippers, and the sleeping cap had been flung about the room. Miss Fayette, naked as the day she was born and oblivious to all, stood at one corner of the canopied four-poster bed. Weeping, she embraced the corner pillar as if it were a whipping post or an object of love.

Tracy said the only words that came to his mind: "Miss Fayette, honey, don't you know you gon' catch your death of cold?"

Miss Fayette looked at Tracy and in the same instant leapt and screamed as if she had been hit by lightning. Then, as he stepped toward her, she fainted into his arms.

Though the greater part of Tracy's stay with Fayette Williams still lay ahead of him, he would always think of that night as the beginning of the final phase, the beginning of the end.

They became lovers. When he deposited her upon her bed, she clung to him in a manner most peculiar for a woman in a faint, and he, being no fool, did what he thought was expected of him. She immediately expressed her appreciation, and one hour led to another.

And, of course, in the months that followed, one night led to another. Fayette always swore that *this* would be the last time, but it never was. With her utopian views, the fact that their affair took place out of wedlock did not bother her, but she nevertheless insisted that it was wrong. Not only was she much too old for him, but there was always the chance that she might have a baby. In point of fact, she would have loved having one, but alas, they did not live in utopia.

Fifteen months after that first night together, they agreed they would have to part. Three times she had been frightened that she was pregnant, and sooner or later she would be. He supposed he loved her in a way, and yet he looked forward to being out on his own. She had a legally certified copy of his manumission made for him to carry, so that she could keep the original for him, safe in her bank strongbox. She made him promise that he would write to her from time to time and even come back and see her if he could manage.

He did write to her, and he did come back to visit. Each of the next three summers he stayed with her for a few weeks. They made love, he nursed her through the period of pregnancy fears, and then he was off again. When he returned during the fourth summer, he found that the house had been sold and that Fayette had gone to live with relatives in Boston. Their correspondence grew increasingly desultory, and before long no more letters were exchanged.

Life was not always easy, but he did better than merely survive. The two hundred fifty dollars with which he had arrived at Fayette Williams' house was his stake. He returned to Cincinnati and got a job sweeping up in a gambling house, and before long, faro and blackjack held no mysteries for him. Poker, however, was his favorite game, and he sharpened his skill by playing for pennies with the other black help. When he felt he was ready, he tested that skill on small-time white gamblers—a handful of cards and a stack of chips knew no color line—and he won. After that, he lived by the cards, playing nightly and building his stake steadily higher. At the age of twenty-one, he got into his first blood-rich game, and he walked away from the table twelve thousand dollars richer.

Then it was the River—the raw world of side-wheelers and hard-drinking captains and keen-eyed pilots, of cotton planters, thieves, slaves, entertainers, whores, dockhands, and gamblers like himself. He won consistently, but winning was not always a guarantee of survival. The color line might disappear over a deck of cards, but it had a way of reappearing when a certain kind of white man lost to a black. Tracy might clip some sucker for an easy thousand or two, but then he frequently had the problem of making a getaway. He never cheated—he could have, but he had no need to—but more than once he had to face an accuser, and more than once he came close to getting shot.

Thus he was happy when he at last got a chance to manage a Louisville gambling house. There he had far more control over any situation that might arise, and his chances of living to a grand old age were distinctly increased. He quickly built a reputation as an honest gambler and an excellent manager, and a year later, this led to his being offered the job of organizing and running a casino aboard the *Duchess of Cairo*. He was reluctant to return to the river, but the offer was tempting, and he figured that a floating casino could not be much different from one on dry land. He took the job and did it well, and soon his control was extended to six more boats.

Eleven years had passed since he had been freed. He was, after a fashion, a success. He had his place in the world, a certain power and a certain privilege. He had no illusion that he had all the privileges of a white man—this evening he had received a stinging reminder from Ethan that he did not—but many a white man might envy him. And, though no white man could ever conceive of the fact, there were those with whom Tracy would not dream of trading places.

Why should he? They were trash, garbage, worse than slaves. And he was Tracy Carter, Prince of the River and master of his own domain.

And, he reminded himself, Ethan Flynn was in that domain right now.

He took one last look at the lights on the docks, one last sniff of the air, and he headed for the gambling lounge.

chapter three

"Honey," Ethan Flynn said, "you got something pretty in them bags you can put on? Something you can wear in a riverboat gambling lounge?"

"They'll be mighty wrinkled."

He thought he detected a hint of Creole accent in the four words. "So you can talk after all," he said.

The girl gave him a brief smile and bent down over one of her bags.

"From New Orleans?" he asked.

"Yes. Will they let me into the gambling lounge with you?"

"They may not know it, but they're going to. I want to show you off. I reckon our gambling friend, Mr. Carter, won't have no objections."

He felt a sickness in the pit of his stomach when he thought of Tracy, a sickness that was eleven years old. He wondered again, as he had thousands of times before, if that black boy had ever actually rammed it into Hannah. In one way, it didn't matter whether he had or not. The important thing was that five people besides himself had seen the two of them naked together. There had been five other witnesses to the fact that his woman had been kissing and caressing a nigger stud.

Well, two of those witnesses were dead now, one of malaria and the other of gunshot wounds, but that left the Colbys and Follett. They knew. They knew what Hannah had been doing, and they undoubtedly believed she had done worse. None of them had ever said a word about it to him, but there it was. They knew.

He had often wished them dead.

He remembered how stunned he had felt after reporting to Addison Carter. There had been nothing more he could do, and a kind of shock had set in. He had been amazed, too, to find that he still planned to marry Hannah if she would have him. She might not have her virginity, but she still had four of the richest plantations in the Delta, and he had counted on owning them for too long to give them up.

There had been snickers and whispers about the community, but they had soon died away, as fresher, richer scandal had captured the imagination. He could never forget what had happened—nor did he want to—but he could marry the girl without too great a feeling of shame for what she was. That is, he could until their wedding night.

"Ethan? . . . What's wrong?"

"Nothing."

"Did I disappoint you?"

"Of course not, darling."

He knew perfectly well that many a virgin reached her wedding night without the physical evidence of her virginity, but he had hoped for that evidence, had somehow even expected it, against all reason. If she had proved to be a virgin, *he,* at least, would have known that she had not been taken by that nigger, no matter what five other witnesses might think. But now he was once again obsessed by the thought that a common black slave boy had robbed him of what should have been his.

The obsession, the sickness, had continued over the years, and in an odd way, he welcomed it: it freed him from responsibility. He could always tell himself that Hannah's behavior on a summer afternoon many years ago had justified his own behavior ever since. From the day Hannah's father had died and Ethan had assumed full control of the Carter holdings, he had lived exactly as he pleased, Hannah be damned, and he always would until the day he died.

And now, after all these years, he had at last caught up with the black boy.

It was time to settle accounts, he decided, time to settle once and for all. He had been robbed of his woman's honor by a nigger and of the nigger's life by old Addison, and it was time he settled with the nigger and Hannah both. He had no idea as yet how he would go about it, but there had to be a way.

However, he had other things in mind for the rest of the night. He enjoyed the curve of Alexandria's buttock and thigh through the taut white dress as she squatted over her bags. From one of them she drew a pair of red shoes, a red garter, and a carefully packed gown of red silk. When she unfolded the gown and held it up for his inspection, it was in surprisingly good condition.

"Fine, honey," he said. "Put it on."

The cabin, though a good one, was cramped—most cabins on riverboats were small—and as Alexandria stripped off her dress, he could have reached out and touched her. He wanted to, but something made him refrain. Her earrings, necklace, and bangles glittered against her rich flesh, and her breasts trembled and swung as she leaned forward and drew the red garter up on the graceful curve of a brown thigh. She showed no more self-consciousness now than she had earlier in the evening when the crowd had inspected her; some sense of dignity made her refuse to feel embarrassed.

I'll take that away from her, Ethan thought, his desire for her flaring, and he was tempted to take her right now—to teach her the kind of master he was and what he expected from her. But no, that could wait. He wanted to gamble, and he would be seeing Tracy again, and he found that wenching slowed his wits. He wanted to keep a clear head. Later, when it didn't matter, he could lock her up naked in the cabin and do as he pleased with her for the rest of the trip.

She lifted the red gown over her head, and reluctantly he watched it slide down her arms and over her shoulders and cover her. His fingers trembled slightly as he assisted her by fastening the hooks at the back of the gown. He wanted her more every minute; it had been a long time since he had looked forward so much to having a woman. But anticipation was part of the pleasure.

He fastened the last hook and leaned forward to speak into her ear. "Later," he murmured.

"Yes, master?"

"Do you know what I'm going to do to you later?"

"Yes, master."

"No, you don't. You don't begin to know. . . ."

She should have been mine, Tracy thought, and he knew he had to have her. One way or another. If he failed, Ethan Flynn would have taken something \besides a woman away from him.

"Do you want to stay with him?" he asked Alexandria, his voice low.

"Do I have a choice?" she asked in return.

"You might."

Alexandria looked across the smoky room at Ethan Flynn, who sat at a blackjack table. The tables were bathed in light, and the corners of the room were in darkness.

"This little brown girl don't know much," she said after a moment, "but she knows something about men. And that one's going to be a cruel master." Sometimes she spoke correctly, he noted, and sometimes she lapsed into a simplified slave idiom; but however she spoke, her voice had a husky, dulcet Creole quality, and he loved its music.

"That bet should have been mine, Alexandria. *You* should have been mine."

"I know," she said. "I wish I was."

In some bleakly sane back corner of Tracy's mind, he knew that what he was about to attempt was suicidal, and he was both terrified and jubilant at his own temerity. He knew very well that a failed attempt to take Alexandria would result, at the very least, in his own further humiliation. And a successful attempt could have even worse results—God only knows what vengeance a man like Ethan Flynn might take. But if there had been any doubt that he would try, those words—*I wish I was*—would have swept them away. Now, it seemed to him, he had no choice.

Without another word, he left Alexandria sitting in her chair in a dark corner and wandered about the room from table to table. While Ethan tried his hand with the bones, he went into the bar, then checked on the cashier's desk. He spent a quarter-hour watching Ethan and making a few side bets of his own. Several plans filtered through his mind, and he settled on none but discarded none. As in the play of the cards, he would know the proper move when the moment arrived.

"Not bad," he said, when Ethan showed signs of tiring of the dice.

"What do you mean, not bad? I'm getting bored with winning."

"We like winners, Mr. Ethan. Keep it up, and we'll make a professional of you yet."

Ethan gave Tracy a quick hard look, and Tracy knew he had played his first card correctly. By striking at Ethan's vanity, he had gained the man's full attention. It was very difficult, after all, to take a sucker who would not pay attention to you.

"I can go into any casino in the country," Ethan said after a moment, "I can buck the house odds, and I can walk away with your money. I have my bad nights, but I'm way ahead, boy, and you better know it."

"Good," Tracy said, "good! As I say, we like winners—"

"But all you do is collect rent on the tables. You sit back and pick up your percentage. You call that gambling? Boy, what do you mean, you're going to make a professional out of me?"

"No offense, Mr. Ethan. I just meant that you're mighty good."

"Anytime you want to lose a little at poker, just let me know."

Tracy rapidly examined poker as a possibility. No, it

would take too long, and too many things could go wrong at the last moment.

"I'll do that," he said politely. "But meanwhile pay a little more attention to the odds on your bets, Mr. Ethan. Just because you're winning is no reason to get careless. And it's not professional."

Tracy turned away and quickly walked into the bar, half expecting to feel Ethan Flynn's heavy hand fall on his shoulder. Even for the free and easy gambling world in which he ruled, it had been a dangerous way to speak to any white man, let alone an Ethan Flynn. Yet he was smiling. Actually, he reflected coolly, he had seen Ethan make only two or three mistakes in the time he was playing, and that was not at all bad for an amateur. He had seen professionals do worse.

Five minutes later Ethan joined him in the bar. He grinned broadly at Tracy. "Can't take it, huh?"

"How's that, Mr. Ethan?"

"Still burning. About the wench. Because I took the bet away from you and then won it."

Tracy laughed. "Maybe so. But I was serious when I said we like winners. And when I said you were good."

"But not professional."

"Well, you see," Tracy said hesitantly, "we like to keep a close eye on the professional gamblers, whether they win or lose, and we learn to spot them pretty easy—"

"But you didn't mark me for a professional, you're saying. Stop pussyfooting, nigger boy, and tell me how you spot a professional."

"Well, there's nothing much to it. It's just telling the sheep from the wolves, same as you do, Mr. Ethan, every time you go to a table. The sheep always tell themselves they've got a streak of luck coming up, or that they got God's own hunch breathed in their ear. . . . But the wolves always know the odds. And their winning streaks aren't wishful thinking."

"And you put me down as one of the sheep."

"Now, I didn't quite mean to do that, Mr. Ethan—"

"You put me down as one of the sheep even though I've already taken almost a thousand dollars off your tables. Sounds to me like you talk a lot better game than you

100

play, black boy. How'd they ever come to put a nigger like you in charge of a gambling lounge, anyway?"

Tracy took the question seriously and gave a straight answer. He signaled a whiskey for Ethan, then told how he had worked for a time in a Cincinnati gambling house, how he had taken to the river, how he had managed the Louisville house and had at last arrived on the *Duchess of Cairo*. As he talked, he quickly gathered a small audience. That usually happened—play tended to fall off in the casino when he discussed his trade; for that reason he tried to avoid the subject. Now, however, he welcomed an audience, though he paid no attention to it. His full concentration was on Ethan Flynn.

"And you've learned all the tricks," Ethan said drily.

Tracy shrugged. "I've learned to know when the odds are good and when they're bad, Mr. Ethan, and how to end up on the right end of them. Offer me a bet where it seems I'm sure to win, and I'll take it. Because I'm a professional. Offer it to another man, and he's likely to say, 'There must be a catch to it,' and turn you down." He looked directly at Ethan and added, "Yet he'll go for a sucker bet every time. And he doesn't even know what a bet of pure chance is."

Ethan turned slowly toward Tracy to return his gaze, and there was a shrewd glint in his lazy, frosty eyes. He said, "You've got something in mind, boy."

"A bet where the previous play of the cards or the way the bones are rolled has no effect. If I select one of several objects, and you tell me which one I chose, that's pure chance, and that's real gambling, Mr. Ethan—"

"That's not what I mean. I saw you talking to the girl. You're still aching for a chance to win her, ain't you?"

Tracy looked past Ethan's shoulder toward the far corner where Alexandria sat alone, a dark princess in blood red, to be bartered, sold, or wagered away. Her eyes met his but asked nothing of him. He knew that to set up a wager and win the girl was almost as dangerous as spitting in Ethan Flynn's face. But . . .

"I wouldn't turn it down," he said thoughtfully. "Not a pure-chance gamble where the odds were right."

"What kind of odds?"

"Even odds, two to one, one in four—I don't much give a damn, not as long as the right price goes with them."

"No bet," Ethan said, "but what would you say was the right price? Just for the sake of argument."

"She's worth eight hundred, maybe a thousand dollars. I suppose I'd take one chance out of four—"

Ethan shook his head. "Twenty-five hundred."

Tracy looked startled. "Mr. Ethan, you're joking with me! She's pretty fancy, that girl, but she ain't no twenty-five-hundred-dollar wench!" he purposely let some of his old accent back into his speech.

"Twenty-five hundred dollars," Ethan repeated. "She was worth twenty-five hundred to both of us earlier this evening, and she's still worth it to me."

"But that was different. We both knew the half-breed—"

"Not to me, it's no different. I own her—I can peg her value anywhere I want."

Tracy stared at Ethan, and Ethan grinned. He seemed to be gauging Tracy, calculating.

"Well, let's see," he said slowly, doing his own calculating. "If I were to name, let's say, four objects and then try to guess which one of them you would pick . . . that would be a pure-chance gamble. I'd have one chance in four, yet I'd have to put up close to her full market value—"

"I say you'd have to put up twenty-five hundred dollars."

Tracy blinked. "But that ain't—that isn't right, Mr. Ethan. You already pegged her value at twenty-five hundred, and I only got one chance in four to win. Now, that ain't fair—"

"Ain't it?" Ethan asked, grinning.

"No, sir—"

"You're a goddam fool, Tracy, don't you know that? All that talk about being professional and playing the odds, and you forget the one thing you should have learned this evening if you never did before. You forget that the odds don't mean a damn thing if a man wants something bad enough. Now, I know how bad *I* want that wench—how bad do you? *I* say you have to bet twenty-five hundred, so put up or shut up!"

Hooked.

At once a look of uneasiness came into Ethan's eyes. He had never really meant to bet Alexandria, and yet he had done so. And he saw that Tracy was going to accept the wager. And they were being watched, listened to, by a dozen or more people: there was no way to back down. Tracy read it all in Ethan's eyes.

"Well, since you put it that way, Mr. Ethan," he said quietly, gently, "I guess you're on."

There were nights when you knew in your guts that luck was with you, and after a bad beginning, this had become one of them. He had led Ethan by the nose. He had his chance to win Alexandria, and he had the *kind* of bet he wanted. Placing twenty-five hundred dollars on a one-in-four shot for Alexandria bothered him not in the slightest; he would willingly have paid ten thousand dollars or more to take the girl away from Ethan, and from that standpoint, the odds were not at all bad.

Besides, Tracy thought the odds might be better than they looked.

"Like I said, Mr. Ethan, I'll pick four objects. I think I'll just make them numbers, and I'll write them down. . . . Let's go to the cashier's desk."

Tracy led the way, and Ethan followed. So did everyone else in the bar. It seemed that word of their bet had preceded them into the lounge as quickly as the terms had been laid down, and a path was made for them. Alexandria's dark, limpid eyes were much wider than they had been before.

"Do you have a bill of sale for the girl?" Tracy asked.

"If you've got twenty-five hundred dollars."

The money and the bill of sale were handed to the cashier, and Tracy requested two sheets of paper and a pen. Blocking the view of the crowd with his body, he wrote the number *3* in the center of the sheet.

"Remember, always number *three*," the old German gambler had told him years ago in Cincinnati. He had been trying to repay a favor. "It doesn't work for everybody, and it won't work for you if you don't do it absolutely correctly. I don't know why it works—some peculiarity of the human mind, perhaps. If I were an ignorant man, I would say it was magic—or just a gambler's touch. All I really know is that it worked three out of four times for the man who taught me. For me, it has never failed."

The German had just taken three hundred dollars from Tracy on this same wager.

Tracy had learned that many a gambler had one special wager that he seldom lost, a wager saved for special moments. This one was his. He had lost the third time he had tried it; five other times he had won. He had no idea if he had won because of "some peculiarity of the human mind" or because of his "gambler's touch" or through sheer good luck. When he won, he always felt exactly as he did when he had made a pass at craps, so perhaps luck was the answer. The odds against a shooter making a pass at craps were greater than those he faced now, yet he had made as many as nine passes in a row.

And now he was going to make a pass of sorts. Simple. If he had not felt in his guts that he was going to make it, he would have steered Ethan into some other kind of bet.

He folded the paper carefully. No one but himself had seen the number 3, not even the cashier, and the number didn't show through the layers of paper. He turned to face Ethan. The man's eyes had lost their uneasiness, and he looked at Tracy with amusement.

"Show me your four numbers," he said.

"Not yet. This paper tells the number I think you're going to pick. Someone should hold it for us." Tracy glanced quickly about the room, then back at Ethan. "Why not you?"

He thrust the paper into a pocket of Ethan's vest, and Ethan said, "Why not?"

Tracy turned back to the cashier's desk. On the second piece of paper he very carefully printed the digits 1 through 4. They all sat on the same invisible base line, but each was taller than the last:

$$1\ 2\ 3\ 4$$

He hesitated for an instant. But the feeling was right. The timing, the rhythm, the tempo was right. He turned to Ethan again and held up the sheet of paper.

"Choose," he said.

Ethan smiled.

There was always the chance that Ethan knew of this gambler's trick, knew that he was expected to name three. Perhaps he himself had used it at one time or another. But, except for the man who had taught it to him, Tracy had never met anyone who had used it. He had always kept it in his reserve bag of tricks. . . .

He waited for Ethan to choose.

Ethan said nothing. He merely smiled.

Tracy fought back the impulse to tell Ethan again to choose.

Then he had a horrible feeling that something was no longer quite right. Something had gone amiss, the timing was wrong, the dice were spinning on their corners, not quite able to fall the right way. He had been too confident. He had fallen prey to the disease that made gamblers think losing was impossible. Like any amateur, he had been overwhelmed by a mere wish, a wish to beat Ethan against the odds. Panic built up in him. Was Ethan about to humiliate him again, humiliate him in his own gambling lounge, before all these people, before the girl Alexandria, and —

"Three," Ethan said.

Another pass.

Now Tracy had made six.

"Sorry, Mr. Ethan," he said quietly, keeping his face and voice carefully neutral. He signaled the cashier for the money and the bill of sale, and tried to ignore the sounds of released tension around him and the glitter of Alexandria's brilliant eyes. When he looked at Ethan again, Ethan had taken the sheet of paper from his vest pocket and was staring at the number *3*. His face was pale.

"Would you sign her over to me on the bill of sale, please?" Tracy asked. "I'll give you a receipt if you wish."

"It don't matter." Ethan made a few quick pen scratches on the bill of sale. "You're lucky tonight, nigger."

"Yes, sir, I guess I am. Shall I send for the girl's bags tonight, Mr. Ethan, or wait till tomorrow?"

"Tomorrow. Hell, I ain't done gambling yet." He held out the piece of paper. "And Tracy . . ."

"Yes, sir?"

"There'll be other nights."

Reaching for the bill of sale, Tracy hesitated—and hated himself for doing so. Ethan's words were a threat, of course, but they were hardly unexpected. Tracy had known the risks he was taking by trying to win Alexandria.

He said, "Yes, sir," and took the bill of sale. The other gamblers were returning to their tables. He looked around for Alexandria and found her. Her face was once again an impassive mask. He went to her, took her elbow, and led her toward the door. She followed him without a word.

At the door, Tracy paused and looked around. Ethan, wearing the faintest of smiles, was still staring in their direction, and Tracy felt an irresistible urge to defy the man. He knew the gesture on the part of a black man was unforgivable, that it could very well cost him his life, but he could not resist it: smiling back at Ethan, he held out his right hand, palm up and cupped, and shook it as if he were rattling something.

Ethan's balls.

"Are you out of your mind?" Alexandria asked as they stepped out onto the deck and into the night. "Don't you know that man gon' kill you for that?"

"He isn't going to kill anybody," Tracy said. The lights about the docks still shone like stars, and the air had never been more spicily perfumed. "This is my country, here on the *Duchess,* and you're my woman now, and *Mister* Ethan can go to hell."

The girl began to laugh.

Then they were both laughing, and the laughter was uncontrollable. Alexandria bent double. Tracy had not laughed so hard since he was a child. They staggered along the deck, falling against the wall and the railing and struggling to keep from collapsing altogether. They fell against each other and reeled apart. Laughter twisted and tore and pained them, and each time it died it immediately started all over again.

When they reached his cabin, he had regained a measure of control, and he managed to unlock the door. Inside, a little light filtered in through the window. Tracy closed and bolted the door, then carefully lighted and adjusted a lamp. Jesus, he thought, what *would* Ethan do about tonight? It was hard to believe he'd just forget—

The thought broke off as he looked around just in time to see Alexandria draw her dress over her head and fling it aside. She kicked off her shoes. Naked except for her jewelry and her red garter, she bounced onto the bed. She lifted the gartered leg and extended her arms toward him.

"You won me," she said. "Take me!"

The *Duchess of Cairo* was delayed a day for repairs, but the following morning she began a fast three-day run to New Orleans. She was big, and she looked clumsy, but when the races began, signaled by a whistled challenge, she was more than able to hold her own. Tracy had won many a dollar on her against faster-looking boats.

He spent his nights in the gambling lounge, most of the time at a poker table. The old game had come up the river from New Orleans and was rapidly becoming the most popular card game in the country. It had been adapted to the fifty-two card pack and was spawning dozens of variations, but it remained a game of judgment and bluff. It was regarded as a man's game, and no woman ever sat down at the table.

Ethan appeared in the lounge every evening.

"You took my wench, black boy—let's see if I can take some of your money."

He appeared to have accepted the loss of Alexandria, and he made no attempt to win her back. At the poker table, he was a good-natured yet hard, shrewd player, and he took more money away with him than Tracy did. That was quite acceptable to Tracy, whose main concern was to run a quiet, honest, profitable casino rather than to make a killing at cards every night. When he was at work, Ethan was just one of the customers.

It was sometimes dawn before Tracy returned to his

cabin, and as he pulled off his clothes and slid into bed, he would still be seeing aces, deuces, and one-eyed jacks. And each time Alexandria would rouse up and give him a sleepy smile.

"Have a good night, master man?"

"Busy."

"Head still whirling 'round?"

"Something terrible. Think you can make it stop?"

"You know I can."

She could and did.

When he awakened, it was almost noon, and a black boy brought food to his cabin. He never ate in the kitchen or with the black help slave or free; it was his habit to eat alone. Now, of course, he had Alexandria with him, his first woman in a long time and one of the very few he had had steadily, and he made the most of the situation. Whenever he was not working, he was with her. They ate together, slept together, pleasured together. The afternoons were spent lounging about the cabin and lying abed in each other's arms.

"You gon' keep me, master man?" she asked on the first afternoon. She was almost catlike in her way of curling up against him, and her voice was a husky purr.

"I just might."

"Whatever you do, don't sell me to that Mr. Ethan. He talks soft, but he is a-a-aye bastard."

"Why should I sell you to anyone? You didn't cost me anything."

They both laughed.

"What you gon' do with me, then?"

"I get tired of you, I'll just kick your tail out."

They laughed again, and she rubbed her bare buttocks. "Poor tail. Tail is all I got, a whore like me."

"You a whore, Alexandria?"

She nodded. "I never sold it, but I sure been sold. And if I ever get free and get me some money, I'm going to open me the lushest, plushest, most expensive cathouse in the whole Delta."

"That your life's ambition?"

She shrugged. "It's what I know how to do."

"How did you learn?"

"Hell, I was brought up in a cathouse. Sold into one when I was eight and out again when I was twelve. Before that, I was just another cane-chewing pickaninny, and I don't know who my mama or papa was. But that cathouse was nice, the absolute best in New Orleans, full of black and white and high yellers and tans, and those gals treated me good. 'Cept for one or two, they weren't mean like most whores—maybe because they were rich. And they taught me everything. How to talk, how to dress, and how to run the lushest and plushest and most expensive. I'm smart, master man, and by the time I was twelve, I really knew. I also learned all the ways of making pleasure with a man."

"I believe you."

She gave him a quick kiss and a tickle. "Sugar, you don't even know yet."

"How'd you come to be sold out of the house?"

"Well, there was a nice old Creole gentleman used to come there. Was about seventy years old and couldn't do much but watch, but I liked him and he liked me, and I could get him going better than anyone else. So he bought me, which was fine with me. But of course I didn't have the fun and the easy time I expected. Not that it was hard times—I just slept in the same room with him and made him happy when I could, and the rest of the time I was a maid. The last year I never even touched him. He caught me pleasuring with the Spanish houseboy, and he said I could as long as he could watch."

She shook her head, and her eyes were thoughtful. "Can't you just hear some fine white lady saying, 'You see there? That black wench got no shame at all. An animal, that's what she is, an animal! Sounds like she's bragging about her life in a house of fallen women. Sounds like she's proud she can give pleasure to an old Creole gentleman. She don't mind at all telling you how she let that old gentleman watch when she was taking the houseboy.' Well, that lady is right. I got no shame. How the hell can I afford shame? You take what they give you in this life and do the best you can with it. So I *am* proud I can run a

109

house. I *am* proud I give pleasure to my nice old gentleman. And if that makes me an animal, then I am goddam proud to be an animal."

Tracy shushed her and ran a finger down her spine.

"Your gentleman sold you?" he asked after a minute.

She shook her head. "He died when I was sixteen. His relatives sold me to a friend of theirs, a Tennessee man. He said he needed me for a trained maid. Hell, that wasn't what he needed me for."

Tracy laughed.

"No, really," she said, "not what you thinking. But almost. He used me for a maid all right, just like my Creole gentleman, and he used me for his own pleasure now and then. But mostly I was for his guests. He was my richest master yet, and every now and then, some governor or senator or suchlike would visit him, and I was for them. You'd be surprised, the important people I gone down on my back for. You believe me?"

"Why not? *Some*body's got to go down for governors and senators and suchlike."

"Pigs, most of them. Hardly a one I woulda chose for myself. But I learned to stop thinking and to get what pleasure I could. I've had pretty easy living, really, not like some poor field hand. Lost two or three babies, had one that lived and got sold. Don't miss it, because I never got to know it, but I sometimes wonder what happened to it. Yeah, I had a lot easier living than most black girls."

"Your Tennessee master sold you?"

"Sold me to that Mr. Cheer. Master got married to one of those fine white ladies I was telling you about. 'That black wench is such an animal! She's got to go!' That lady, she hated my guts, and I bet she's no good in bed at all. Mr. Cheer bought me, and you know what happen to me then."

She yawned, rolled as far as the bed would allow, and adjusted her position so that she could look into his eyes. "What about you?" she asked. "You born free?"

"No. My master set me free. Years ago."

Her eyes widened. "Why'd he do that?"

"Because I killed a man. My best friend."

"You lie!"

"No, I'm not lying. My friend went crazy somehow. Nearly killed a girl—the same girl Mr. Ethan Flynn later married—"

"That Hannah you talked about?"

"That's right. Anyway, I killed him before he could kill someone else. Some people said he was my father."

Alexandria looked steadily into his eyes. "You're making all this up. . . . No, maybe you ain't. You got a fine sheen like fresh sweat on your face. Maybe you're telling the truth."

"It was a long time ago and doesn't matter anymore."

He closed his eyes and listened to the sounds that filtered into the room from the other parts of the boat and from the docks. Other people were hard at work, and here he was, only half awake, with a girl in his arms. Smart girl. Beautiful girl. Could talk like a field hand or a house nigger or a fine white lady. He had worked hard for this, of course—and how many other black men had risen as he had? How many whites? . . .

"Alexandria?"

"Yes, master man."

"Am I really your master man?"

"Guess so. You won me."

"Then you listen to me. You're not ever again going to pleasure a man when you don't want to. You don't do *anything* with *any* man when you don't want to. You understand me?"

A long minute passed. He felt her lift her head, felt her breath on his cheek. "Don't have to do anything with any man?"

"That's right."

"Not even with you?"

"Not if you don't want to. Not even with me."

Distant laughter, chatter, and the creakings and clatterings of life and work continued to filter into the cabin from the afternoon beyond the locked door. Tracy almost dozed off. But then he felt something that brought him instantly awake.

"Come to life, master man," Alexandria said huskily. "You gon' get pleasuring like you never got before in your whole life. . . ."

A steamboat trip was always something of a risk—sinkings and engine explosions were common—but late on a sunny afternoon the *Duchess of Cairo* paddled along the New Orleans waterfront, a five-mile stretch thick with steamers. Tracy pulled himself out of bed, got dressed, and went out on deck to have a look.

The lower deck was crowded with freight and with deck passengers. Many of the deck passengers were slaves who had been sold south, and they had made the trip in chains. If the *Duchess* had sunk, the slaves would probably have had the least chance of all the passengers to survive. Tracy shook his head and felt sorry for them.

But he had his own problems, he told himself. He wanted to check on two of his other boats while he was here—he had grown distrustful of a dealer on one of them, and he wanted to see if the accounts on the other were now being kept more to his liking.

Evening fell. The boat emptied far more rapidly than it had filled up, and it soon had a deserted feeling about it. Still, there would be some business in the gambling lounge tonight.

As always, he ate in his cabin with Alexandria, and he told her that he probably would not be working late.

"You've had a nice trip?" she asked.

"If you made it any nicer, woman," he said, "you'd kill me."

"You're not tired of me?"

He proved that he was not, then he dressed for business and went to the lounge. For the first time since Memphis, Ethan Flynn was not there; he had left the boat. Tracy put in a busy four hours, then headed back for his cabin.

On the way, he paused to see what he could of the lighted waterfront. All waterfronts were different, yet all were the same. He wondered if he dared go ashore tomorrow. Probably he should not, but at times confinement to the boat gave him a feeling of being smothered. Not that he had minded the confinement with Alexandria . . .

He leaned out over the rail, looking. Not much to see, really. Nothing that he hadn't seen dozens of times before . . .

He brought his hands up too late. He heard the scuffling of their feet at the same time that he saw shadows move, and he hunched, lowered his head, and raised his arms instinctively. He hardly had time to be afraid before the back of his head exploded. His knees began to buckle, and he strained to stay on his feet and strike back. His head exploded again, and he found himself on his knees with his head pulled back. Something was jammed between his teeth. A bitter fluid poured over his tongue, and he gagged.

His head exploded a third time.

Darkness came over him like a velvet blanket.

chapter four

And then the velvet blanket was hot, steaming hot, and filthy-sticky, and pain awakened like a small point of flame surging up in a vast darkness.

He had no idea where he was, and he didn't want to know. He didn't want to think. Any thought, any movement, might make the pain flare up higher. He wanted to stay in the darkness, to drop back down again, far down into it.

But he couldn't go back. The pain grew, throbbed, increased in sudden leaps, and he heard himself whimper. He tried to lie still, but a tremor ran through him, and he knew he was no longer on the deck of the *Duchess* nor even in his cabin. He seemed to be lying on bare earth—earth that had been pounded hard. He was lying face down, and he could feel it and smell it.

He groaned and rolled over onto his back, keeping his eyes tightly closed. A hand rested lightly upon his forehead for a few seconds and then withdrew. He tried to swallow and found it almost impossible, so painfully dry were his mouth and throat.

"Tracy?" someone whispered.

The pounding in his head got worse and in some way linked itself with the dryness of his mouth and throat. Then he became aware that something was happening in his belly: a growing nausea. He tried again to swallow, and he retched. The nausea grew like a poisonous flow within him and became one with the painful throat and the pounding head.

Involuntarily, he stirred again, and he became aware that his feet were bare. He moved his hands and found that he wore no shirt. He seemed to have on only the scrappy remains of an old pair of pants.

"Tracy? Tracy?" The hand moved on his forehead again, then went away.

The air he was breathing was hot, fetid, and rank. It smelled of sweat, feces, urine, vomit; every lungful was poisonous. He heard stirrings around him, and whispers and groans and murmurings. A child began to cry.

He opened his eyes but shut them again immediately. What little light there was—falling in thin streaks as if it were coming in between spaced boards—hurt his eyes and increased the aching and the nausea.

There was no point any longer in trying to avoid thought. He was awakening, and in a slow, painful, crippled way, his intelligence was insisting on its function. It tried to understand what had happened, where he was, how he had come to be here. He had been in his cabin . . . no . . . at the poker table . . . no . . . out on deck . . . yes? . . . yes, on deck . . . and someone had attacked him. . . .

"Tracy?"

Slowly he opened his eyes again. The effort was so painful, that at first he could not make sense of the face that was over his. It was distorted. . . .

"Alexandria," he whispered after a moment. A whisper was the most he could accomplish; his throat felt lacerated.

"You was unconscious so long, you scared me."

"What? . . ."

"They gave you poison of some kind, I reckon. Same as they did me. Hit me, then made me drink that stuff."

Yes, he remembered that. He had found himself on his knees, his head pulled back, and someone had poured a bitter liquid down his throat. That, as well as the blows he had absorbed, would account for his pounding head. It would also account for his painful throat and his nauseous stomach.

"Are you all right?" he asked.

"Better than you."

"But who? . . ."

"I don't know. I never got a chance to look. Somebody knocked at the door; said you sent him. I thought it was a boy with something to eat or drink." She laughed painfully. "I guess it was. Something to drink. I open the door, and *boom!* they grab me and hit me. Then one's got me round the head so I can't see, and the other's making me drink some stuff. I got sick right away—maybe that's why it don't hurt me the way it do you. But I go off to sleepy land like a baby anyway, and when I wake up, here I am."

"And where are we?"

"Look and see, master man. Look and see."

With her help, he managed to sit up; the very effort was sickening. Now for the first time he looked around at the source of the whispers and groans and murmurings he heard.

Black people. Like himself. A hundred fifty, perhaps two hundred, crowded into the crude shed. Old people, a very few, gray and bent. A number of infants, most of them naked. Some young couples huddled together. Several pregnant women, one apparently on the verge of labor. Field hands, both male and female. A few who looked as if they might have been skilled craftsmen, artisans. Most wore one or two items of the simplest clothing, plus brogans, and a few wore the soiled remnants of very good clothes. Alexandria, he saw, wore what appeared to be one of her own dresses, now badly stained. He remembered she had said she had been sick.

Black people.

He knew what they were and why they were here. And he knew that he was one of them. The fact that he should not have been here was irrelevant. The fact that he had been beaten and drugged and brought here with his woman by force was irrelevant. Every single person in this shed might have pressed a claim that he should not have

116

been here, that his bondage was unjust and immoral, a crime against humanity. But still they were here, and Tracy was one of them.

He was a slave again.

PART THREE

PART THREE

chapter one

Life had the quality of a nightmare.

He heard the doors of the shed scrape open, and light flooded painfully into the shed. He found Alexandria helping him to his feet; his head pounded, and he reeled, and he had to lean on her. They went with the others out into the fenced-in yard. There he found that they were expected to pick up wooden shingles, which were used as plates. As they filed past a number of great iron pots, cornmeal mush with hogfat was ladled out to them, and they ate with their fingers or with sticks. Afterwards they filed by pumps, where they were to wash the shingles as quickly as possible and to take a quick drink of water.

Tracy could not eat. When he reached the pump, some instinct made him gulp water greedily until he was pushed roughly on by a white driver. He returned with Alexandria to the shed, sank to the earthen floor, and was half asleep again before the doors ground closed.

When he next awakened, he was no longer sick, but both his brain and his stomach were numb.

"How long have we been here?" he asked Alexandria.

"Been a day since you first woke up. I woke up the day before. Guess we been here two, three days now."

The third time he awakened, his stomach complained painfully of hunger. He ate mush from a shingle along with the others.

The nightmare quality continued. He was Tracy Carter, and what was he doing here? He was no slave and hadn't been since boyhood. And even then he had never been subjected to anything like this. He had heard of these places where slaves were bought and sold, but they weren't part of *his* life. Even as a child he had been privileged compared to these blacks. He had never before in his life eaten off of a shingle. *What was he doing here?*

He had known that New Orleans was not the safest place for him, but no place was entirely safe for any man. And it was hardly unheard of for a free black man—even one from the North—to be taken captive and sold into slavery. There was a criminal trade in black men just as there was in any other valuable property. Moreover, the burden of proof that he was free lay on the black man. But still Tracy found it almost impossible to absorb the fact that he was here, a slave among slaves, waiting to be sold.

When his brain began to function properly again, he approached a white driver.

"Sir, who's the master around here? I've got to see him, sir—"

The answer was the whip against the back of his thighs, and he had all he could do to keep from raising a clenched fist. But that, he knew, was the worst thing he could do. The next time the opportunity arose, he went to a black driver, one who was almost certainly a slave himself.

"Who's the master around here? I've got to see him."

The man grinned, showing foul teeth. "You want to complain about your grits?"

"No, I want to know how I got here. I want to know who brought me here."

"I guess you can't remember, you was so sick. But I remember."

"Then who—"

"Don't know, never saw them before. Some white men, natcherly, they sold you to the Colonel."

"I want to see the Colonel—I've got to explain to him —you see, those white men stole my woman and me—"

"Who your master?"

"We didn't have a master. We were free—"

"You ain't got no big important master, the Colonel don't give a damn." The man grinned again, more broadly than ever. "You ain't free now."

"But I've got to talk to him. I've got to explain—"

"I told you, he don't give a damn. Don't ask me to talk up for you, I got no yearning get my ass whipped. You black, you slave, and you always gon' be slave."

The driver, losing interest, turned away, but Tracy still wanted information.

"These white men who brought my woman and me, how many of them were there? Did they bring any other— slaves—at the same time?"

"Three white men. No, I don't know if they bring any other. Now, you clean your shingle. We not supposed talk to you."

Tracy looked carefully through the crowd in the shed, but he saw no other blacks from the *Duchess*. Apparently only he and Alexandria had been taken. Possibly other victims had been taken to other slavers, but it seemed likely to him that there was another explanation.

"Alexandria, it's mighty funny, my being taken from the deck of the boat and you from my cabin and no other black from the *Duchess* stolen. There were a number of others they could have taken."

"You mean your old friend and my recent master had something to do with it."

"You think so, too?"

"I thought so all along. He planned on having me in his cabin all the way from Memphis to New Orleans. In a way, he took me away from you. Only you took me back again, and it's you I've been pleasuring with. And you're a black boy and him a white man. He ain't the kind of white man to let that pass. He's the kind would hate your guts for that."

"He's hated me for years."

"Well, there you are, Sugar. Now you know who put us here."

"When I catch up with him, I'll kill him."

Alexandria touched his shoulder and smiled. She said nothing, but the touch and the smile and the look in her eyes told him the words she was holding back.

After the days and the nights on the *Duchess of Cairo,* they knew each other. And he knew that she pitied him now.

The shed seemed to be a kind of warehouse. Each day a certain number of blacks were taken out, some of them never to be seen again. Those who returned told of auctions. Some returned weeping, to tell of their families having been sold away from them. Most of those who returned wanted to say as little as possible about what had occurred wherever they had been.

It rained. The roof leaked, and water was blown between the boards of the walls. The floor quickly turned to mud, and there was no way of avoiding it; the shed turned into one gigantic hog wallow, and those whose clothing and bodies had some last vestige of cleanliness completely lost it. Muddy, they went out into the rain twice a day to collect mush on their shingles and eat it before the torrent could wash it away. Then, if they wished, they were allowed to go to lime-filled ditches to relieve themselves. There were no separate toilet facilities, merely the ditches over which men and women squatted together, while their guards stood by watching and making obscene remarks.

The sun came out again, and the shed reeked worse than ever. Never before, not in any barnyard or stable, had Tracy ever experienced such a foul, sickening, obscene smell. It was as if human beings, when treated worse than cattle, had an odor that became infinitely worse. The mud, the crowded conditions, and most of all the odor were as degrading as the shingles they ate from and the latrine trenches they used, and with a kind of horror, Tracy made an ironic discovery about himself. *He would actually be glad when at last he was sold.*

Planned or not, the steady treatment of degradation was having its effect—and within just three days of his regaining full consciousness. The nightmare world he was now in was becoming the real world. Nothing could be more im-

124

mediate, more desperate, more real than this world. Everything else, everything he had experienced during the past eleven years, had been at best a pleasant dream. . . .

The doors of the shed opened, and through them were thrust replacements for those slaves who had been sold. A white captain with whip-armed drivers at his sides walked through the room looking for this or that slave. "The cobbler! Where's that cobbler, was brought in here yesterday. Got a good new master for you, cobbler!" A small boy defecated in a corner. Men and women lost themselves in sex in the night. A fourteen-year-old girl was dragged weeping away from her family. Later she was returned naked, blank-eyed, and mute, unable to tell what had been done to her. The blood told.

Ethan Flynn entered the cafe by way of the door from his hotel. As he had expected, a tall cadaverous man dressed in white sat at one of the tables, a drink before him. He smiled at Ethan and lifted a hand. Ethan returned the smile and the salute. They were old acquaintances—old enough that the cadaverous man could, with some confidence, signal a boy that he wanted two more of the same he had been drinking. Ethan sat down at the table with him.

"Having a good visit?" the man asked.

"Fair enough. I won four hundred on cockfights last night."

"Sorry I couldn't be there."

"Oh, the birds were nothing special. It was just that I was picking the right ones, and I had a fool to cover every bet I made."

The cadaverous man grinned. "You always were good at finding fools to cover your bets."

"When it comes to gambling, I'm just a poor amateur, Tyler," Ethan said with a thin smile, "or so I've been told. But I've also been told that the real professionals like winners."

Tyler laughed. "Yes, I suppose they do, at that. In house games, at any rate. Winners help bring in losers. Me, I've always preferred a private game."

"So do I."

"I hope we can arrange something before you leave?"

"I think we can."

"How about tonight?"

"Ethan shook his head. "I've heard about some knifers I want to see."

"Fights? Ethan, there's been a lot of disapproval of that sort of thing lately. This ain't the frontier anymore, you know—James Bowie and his kind are dead or dying out. We're civilized now. And they say some niggers got killed in fights just recently—"

"Wish I'd had money on the survivors."

Tyler laughed again, and they lapsed into silence and sipped their drinks. The room was pleasantly dark and cool compared with the brilliantly sunlit outdoors.

"How much longer are you going to want me to keep that pair?" Tyler asked at last.

"Until I head back to the ancestral plantation. Another week or so."

"I can't help wondering just what your game is."

"Game?" Ethan said smiling. "What makes you think I'm up to any game?"

Tyler's thin face took on a mock seriousness, and he waved his long narrow hands in a gesture of denial. "Oh, I don't think that, Ethan, but if I were a suspicious man, I might almost think you'd stolen the pair of them somewhere and were trying to cover your tracks. But that makes no sense, because why would you steal them and pay for them too? Not unless there's something special about them—"

"Tyler, I told you. I just happened to come by when they were delivered to you, and I thought they were a mighty handsome pair, all stretched out there." He did not really expect Tyler to believe him, but he hardly cared one way or the other. "I paid you a holding fee so that you wouldn't sell them off until I was ready to make my bid. Now, I expect you to keep to our agreement."

"Of course, of course, no question. But when the time comes to sell them, I *am* selling them for the highest bid I can get."

"Certainly you are, that's perfectly right. You just ain't

putting them up for sale until I tell you to. And when you do put them up, you gon' give me every opportunity to make the highest bid. No hanky-pank, now!"

Tyler laughed ironically and said, "No hanky-pank." He played with his glass for a moment, then said, "The wench, that Alexandria. I took a good look at her. You scrape the mud off, and she is really one fancy piece of female. I myself have no special taste for black meat, but *that* bitch—"

"You ain't touched her, I hope."

Tyler looked up, a little surprised at the sharpness, which Ethan had been unable to keep out of his voice. "Of course not. You told me you didn't want her touched."

"And I still don't. Not by you, Tyler, and not by your blacks and not by your white help."

"You would appear to have a real compassion for that pair of niggers."

"That's right, I got a real compassion. Wouldn't want anything to happen to them, anything that might come between 'em, anything at all. Just want 'em left alone. I'm sure they're really enjoying your hospitality in that goddam shed of yours, and I want to keep it that way for a while."

"And you still say you don't even know them? Neither of them means a thing to you?"

"Not a thing. The only thing that matters to me is the agreement we made."

Tyler threw up his hands and shrugged his shoulders. "So be it," he said.

Others were brought to the shed and were later taken away, never to be seen again, but Tracy and Alexandria stayed on. In time, only a handful of elderly and hard-to-sell slaves remained of those who had been there when they arrived, and this seemed to them to confirm their belief that Ethan Flynn had something to do with their bondage.

The crowd within the shed swelled and diminished, swelled and diminished. Each day brought a deeper despair, and one day Tracy found himself pounding on the walls, trying to hammer his way out. In time, guards came and gave him five lashes. They were quite enough. He would never pound on the walls again.

More families were torn apart. Someone among their captors had a particular penchant for abusing very young girls. An old woman died, and that night her husband managed to hang himself from a nail on the wall. Women bore babies, and most of them died. A few men fought to take women, others fought desperately to defend them. One tried to take Alexandria away from Tracy, and he fought for her, remembering his promise that she would never again have to have a man she did not want. To his surprise, when the guards came, it was the other man who was whipped.

That night, lying in the dark with her, and within inches of other sleepers, he wanted her for the first time since their abduction. Until now, he had been utterly without desire. He had never thought there was anything intrinsically degraded or degrading about wanting and taking a woman, but to take Alexandria here and under these circumstances seemed to degrade them both.

Alexandria felt him move beside her and understood his restlessness. "Sugar," she whispered, touching him, "it's all right."

Her touch aroused him further, and he gritted his teeth, yet he could not bring himself to brush her hand away. "No," he forced himself to whisper after a moment, "not here, not like this."

"Nobody gon' know."

"*They* know! That goddam Ethan knows!" He found himself speaking aloud, and there were moans and whimpers from the others around them. "They know all about it, and *it's what they want!*" He felt suddenly that he had struck on some profound and unassailable truth.

"Shush, baby," Alexandria said.

"But don't you understand—"

"Course I understand. But they don't touch me that way, nor you neither. Sugar, you'll feel better, and 'sides, I need you, too."

That persuaded him to roll onto his side toward her, but there was no real pleasure in his taking her, only tension and release, followed by a new and special despair beyond tears. But he pretended to feel better for Alexandria's sake. He lay still in the dust and the hot stinking darkness and at last found sleep.

The next afternoon they were taken from the shed.

The door opened, and two white guards, whips in hand, appeared. They were like black shadows in the sudden light of the doorway. "Tracy and Alexandria," one of them called out, "all right, where's Tracy and Alexandria? Get your black asses on outside."

Hearing their names spoken came as a shock. No one had given them the slightest special attention in the time they had been there—three or four weeks? a month?—and Tracy could not remember having mentioned their names to any of their captors.

"Tracy and Alexandria, goddammit!" the man repeated.

Alexandria tugged nervously at Tracy's arm, and they went to the door. The guard impatiently shoved them out into the glaring sunlight. Tracy could recall no other time when only two people were taken from the shed unless they were females that the guards had taken a fancy to. Usually the slaves were taken out a dozen or more at a time.

The door of the shed was closed again and barred. The guards led them to a pump and trough. "Now, get them rags off and get yourselves clean," the one who had ordered them out of the shed said. "There's a big piece of yeller soap there, and you can pump for each other. See if you can get rid of the stink."

The only alternative to obeying was to be whipped or perhaps killed. There was no place to run to, no place to hide. The area was surrounded by a high board fence, and the gate was closed and no doubt guarded.

"What's the matter, nigger, you don't know what getting clean is? I said get busy at that pump!"

Alexandria was already stripping. Naked, she acted with the same dignity she had exhibited the first time Tracy had seen her in Memphis. One would have thought

129

she had no idea that she was being observed by strangers. Tracy stepped up to the pump and began working the handle for her.

"Jesus, how did I miss this one?" the other guard said, speaking for the first time. He was the younger of the two, and he was staring at Alexandria.

"You missed her because the Colonel gave orders she wasn't to be touched."

"That's why I didn't look for her. Didn't even notice under all that dirt. But if I'd known, I'd said to hell with the Colonel."

"I thought you didn't like 'em over fourteen," said the older guard with disgust.

"Sometimes I do. Hey, think we got time—"

"No."

When Alexandria was done, she took over the pump handle, and Tracy dropped his tattered pants and washed. He was just finishing when a man he had heard referred to as the Captain appeared. The Captain was carrying some clothing, which he handed to the younger guard, and he turned to Tracy. Without preamble, he peeled back Tracy's lips and looked into his mouth.

"Damn good teeth for a nigger," he growled. "Any of 'em hurt, boy?"

"No, sir," Tracy managed to say through a throat suddenly gone dry.

"Lean forward against the pump and spread your legs."

Tracy did as he was told, and the Captain was mercifully swift with his physical examination, prodding him for weaknesses and looking for signs of disease or imperfection. But his hands missed nothing, and Tracy flinched and trembled as they roamed over him. He felt even more humiliated when the Captain gave Alexandria exactly the same examination.

The younger guard giggled and said, "I be glad to do that for you, Captain."

"The only reason we keep *you* here," the captain snapped to the guard, "is because you ain't worth selling." His eyes had never once met Tracy's or Alexandria's.

He took the clothing from the younger guard and handed it to Alexandria and Tracy, a long shift for her and pants and shirt for him. They were torn and worn thin, but they were clean, and they were received almost gratefully.

The Captain led the way through the gate, along a dusty path, and into another compound. The first thing Tracy saw was a crowd of white men—at a glance he thought eighty or a hundred, but there might have been more—most of them watching a wooden platform. There were also a number of blacks, some of them in chains.

"You know what they gon' do?" Alexandria whispered.

"Yes."

"They gon' separate us!"

"Maybe not." Actually, Tracy had very little hope that they would be able to remain together.

A few of the whites were clustered about the back of the platform, and a tall cadaverous man made his way between them to address the Captain.

"What shape are they in?"

"Both of them first class. No hernia, no piles, no nothing. No running sores and never have been. Both got good teeth, too."

"Whip marks?"

"None on the man that show bad. None at all on the woman."

"Good. Get them both up on the platform."

The Captain turned to Tracy and Alexandria. "All right, you two, you heard the Colonel. Get your asses up them steps."

Alexandria led the way up the short wooden ladder that led to the platform, and Tracy saw her hesitate as she reached the top step. He followed her gaze.

If there had remained the slightest doubt in Tracy's mind that Ethan Flynn was responsible for the situation in which he and Alexandria found themselves, it was now gone forever. Ethan was out there in the crowd—waiting for them.

Ethan bought them for twenty-seven hundred dollars.

Afterwards, he bought three more females, all of them close to six feet tall, muscular, big boned. Field hands. Listening to what was said, Tracy gathered that earlier he had purchased two males and five other females.

"You gon' take them with you, Mr. Flynn," the Captain asked, "or you want us to send 'em up?"

"You've got a coffle headed my way in a few days, don't you?"

"Tomorrow."

"Then put boots on 'em and send 'em up. But I don't want a whip used on that Alexandria wench if you can help it. She's mighty fancy, and I want to keep her that way. If you put chains and a collar on her, pad them good so she don't get marked up."

Tracy watched and listened. Ethan looked at him and smiled, but neither gave the other any particular sign of recognition.

"We'll have them on their way to you tomorrow, Mr. Flynn."

They were taken to a different shed for the night. This one was much cleaner and had a board floor, and there were a few blankets on which to sleep. In the morning, they again ate from shingles and were given an opportunity to relieve themselves over open ditches.

Then the coffle was organized. The slaves were tagged and chained together in pairs. Shoes and straw hats were given to those who lacked them. Iron collars were padlocked around necks and attached to each other by long chains. The coffle was made up of several sections of about twenty slaves each, walking two by two. In the main, an attempt was made to keep together those slaves with a common destination, and Tracy and Alexandria were together, though the differences in their heights and strides would make for difficulty in walking.

"Now, we gon' move!" shouted the master of the coffle from astride his mule. "We gon' move fast! The faster we move, the sooner you all can stop walking. You gon' get rest periods, but only if you *move!* If there any trouble, if any you hold us up, we gon' have a special punishment section. And that section is gon' have no boots. That section gon' go barefoot. That section get the whip like they never got it before. You all understand me? You all gon' *move! move! move!* . . . All right, now. Let's move out. *Yo-o-o!*"

But the coffle moved like a sluggish beast, like a huge wounded snake. The sun burned down, and the whip fell. For long periods not a full minute passed without a whip sounding somewhere along the line, and as the day wore on the lashings became more frequent. Every couple of hours there was a few minutes' rest, and then the weary, staggering double line moved on.

Night came. A rest station had been set up on a plantation. The slaves ate, so weary they hardly knew what they were eating. They had precious seconds at a pump and at crude latrines. The lucky ones were then locked up in an old barn and a couple of sheds. The unlucky ones slept in the open air, or tried to, still in their chains.

On their first night, Tracy and Alexandria were among the lucky. They found a scrap of musty hay in the barn loft. The loft was hot and crowded, and the air hardly breathable, but at least the hay was soft, and they were relieved of their chains. Traveling by coffle was a form of torture, but now the torture was over for a few hours.

"Tracy," Alexandria whispered, "we gon' be all right, ain't we?"

"We'll be fine."

"I been thinking. It's all my fault this happening to you."

"Don't be foolish. I told you, Ethan Flynn started hating me years ago."

"What you think he gon' do to us when we get there?"

"I don't know. Nothing. Don't worry about it. Better sleep, little girl."

"Yes, master man."

For a while, Tracy thought he was too weary and uncomfortable for sleep. His mind raced erratically among memories of the last few weeks, from discomfort to humiliation to pain. But then, abruptly, he passed from one nightmare realm into the other.

chapter two

Hannah Flynn stood on her front veranda and watched the coffle approaching on the road. The Carter mansion, her home, was placed almost a hundred yards back from the road, but her eyes were good; thus far she could make out two sections of at least twenty slaves each, followed by a third of about a dozen. *Poor goddam devils,* she thought. *Poor goddam suffering niggers.*

She was a tall woman with medium-weight bones, broad in the shoulders and the pelvis. Her thick black hair fell unkempt to her shoulders, where it appeared to have been casually hacked off with a knife. Her face was burned unevenly to a reddish, copper color, and her arms and legs were a deeper brown, the down on them bleached gold by the sun. Her only garment was an old gingham dress that had worn thin and could have been cleaner, and she seldom wore anything else. She was barefoot, and she had the splayed feet of a woman who never wore shoes when she could avoid them. Her lips were full, but the lower tended to hang crudely slack. She always frowned slightly and looked on the world with narrowed eyes. She could have been a beautiful woman; she looked like a petulant child.

At one point on the road, there was access to the carriage path that circled up to the front of the mansion and also to the service path that circled around in back. The two twenty-slave sections of the coffle slowly worked their way past this point. The third section, however, the one with the dozen slaves, came to a halt. And Hannah saw Tom Barclay, for the last several years her overseer, walking along the service path.

Her frown deepened. She watched as Tom talked to a guard who had dismounted from a mule. The guard separated two blacks, a man and a woman, from the coffle, and Tom handed him something that would have been a receipt. The two men talked for another few seconds, and Tom pointed along the road in the direction that the coffle was headed—toward the Flynn plantation. The guard remounted, and the chained slaves began to move again, and Tom headed back toward the slave quarters with the man and the woman. The black couple looked bone-weary, hardly able to lift their feet.

Tears of anger and frustration formed in Hannah's eyes, and she went back into the house. She stamped her way to the office in the west wing and threw herself gracelessly into the chair behind the big oak desk. Her elbows pounded down on the desk like hammers.

They had to right to treat her this way. She was supposed to be running this plantation, and she wanted to run it, she wanted to run it right. Christ, she had nothing else to do. Then why didn't Ethan let her run it? Why did he never consult her? He brought in hands and took them away and never said a word, and then Barclay said, "Ma'am, the reason I never mentioned it was I thought you knew." With that go-to-hell look in his eyes, because he didn't like working for a woman. And Enright, the overseer on the Flynn plantation, was even worse. Sometimes she thought they both had more authority over the Carter plantation than she did. And so did they.

She considered having a drink, but she didn't really want one. She often wished she were a drinking woman, but liquor never seemed to help her much. . . . Well, in a little while, she would go out and learn the story on the two new hands.

She tried to concentrate on her accounts but failed. It was almost a relief when she recognized the sound of Ethan's boots in the hallway, and she looked up to see him coming through the door. He was covered with road-dust and sweat, and he grinned at her.

"Looks like I timed it just right," he said. "Got home in the same hour the coffle got here."

Fine, she thought, we'll have it out right now, and she said, "Where the hell do you get off, sending me two more hands without even asking me?"

"That's a nice greeting after two months' absence." Ethen settled himself on a corner of a table where he could grin down at her. "I bring home a dozen slaves, and before you even say welcome, you're raising hell—"

"A dozen! You mean there's more of them?"

"Eight of the biggest damn female field hands you ever saw. And two bucks to keep 'em happy. I figure that's a right generous proportion, four to one. Don't you?"

"I told you before, I ain't going into the slave-breeding business!"

"Oh, ain't you!" Ethan laughed. "Woman, do you know how the price of niggers is going up—"

"I don't care—"

"I paid twenty-seven hundred dollars for the pair that the coffle left here. And you'll never again see the day when you can hire slave labor at a dollar a day—it's going to cost you almost as much as white labor. And the only answer is to do more breeding of our own instead of depending on Virginia and the Carolinas. And the only answer to *that* is at least four goddam bitches to every stud. Am I right?"

"I won't have no part of it—"

"Nobody's asking you—"

"I run this plantation—"

"But I run you!"

Hannah flinched as if she had been struck, and she felt her cheeks flame. Ethan, still sitting on the corner of the table, grinned at her.

"I don't want your—your breeders on this plantation," she said after a moment.

"They ain't yet. There ain't enough quarters for them

here on Carter, so I had them taken up the road to Flynn. But, goddam, woman, you just gon' have to get used to the idea that when I married you, I took over lock, stock, and barrel, same as any other man would. Your ole daddy trusted me, and I got things in my hands—"

"Or if he didn't, you got them anyway."

"Something like that. Now, if you want to run this place, that's just fine with me. *Some*body's got to run it. And I understand your sentimental feelings about it, raised up here and all. And you do a pretty fair job, too."

"Thank you very much."

"It ain't a lady's job; but then . . . you ain't no lady."

Hannah didn't answer. She knew from his words and the way he said them what was coming next. She knew from the hardening of Ethan's eyes, even though he kept on smiling. She had been through this at least a hundred times.

"I said . . . you ain't no lady."

"No," Hannah replied wearily, "I ain't no lady."

"All that touring around Europe, all that fine European education, and it don't count for nothing, does it? . . . Does it?"

"No, it don't count for nothing."

"Jesus. You ought to look at yourself in a mirror. Do you ever look at yourself in a mirror, woman?"

"No." She rested her head on one hand and closed her eyes, hoping he would be done quickly.

"I can see why. You already know what it'd show you. Do you know what you look like, woman?"

"I know."

"Like a slut. Like some poor ignorant white-trash slut, would do a man anything for half a dollar. Butt spreading like lard and tits showing right through that worn-out dress —Jesus! Like a slut or a sow, that's what. A goddam old sow, straight out of the hog waller."

She felt tears coming to her eyes. She was always surprised to find how deeply he could hurt her, though she had long ago ceased to feel anything like love for him.

"Ain't you got nothing to say?" he asked.

She shook her head.

"No defense, no complaints?"

"No."

"Just like a slut or a sow . . . Yes, sir, all you need is a little something to pleasure your tail now and then, just like a slut or a sow, and you're happy. Ain't that right?"

"You know I—I—I—"

"You what?"

"You know I haven't—I don't—"

"Don't what? Don't get no pleasuring? Now, I find that hard to believe. All the fine black boys you got right here on the plantation, and not a thing to stop you from getting all you want—how many black boys you had in you, woman?"

"I never did. You know I never did—"

"I know a black boy ruined you—"

"He did not! If you think that, why did you marry me?"

"Maybe I didn't think so at first. Or maybe I learned not to give a damn. Hell, maybe I don't give a damn now."

"Then why don't you leave me alone?"

"Maybe I would if you told me the truth. That black boy I caught you with just before you went off to Europe —now, don't tell me you forgotten—he was giving it to you, wasn't he?"

"Can't you ever forget—"

"No, I can't ever forget—why should I? Why don't you tell me about him?"

"But I've told you, he didn't—we didn't—"

"Was he the only one, or were there others? Was he your first? How often did you do it with him, and what all *did* you do? How does a slut like you act with a nigger? Tell me about it, slut—"

"Damn you," she said, fighting hard against the tears, "damn you, damn you, damn you—"

He slapped her—casually and hard and still smiling.

"Watch your language."

"Fuck you."

His laughter was sharp, vicious, triumphant. "You even talk like a slut. But I'll tell you the truth, woman—you always were a pretty dead piece of ass—"

"And you!" Sometimes rebellion flared up explosively, and it did now. "Shall we tell the truth about you? How it

138

took a pig like you to make a sow out of me? How you could never pleasure a real woman because you're not a real man? How all you know is hate and pain—"

He grabbed the front of her shift and pulled her closer. He slapped her again, much harder than the first time. He was still grinning, but his grin was strained, and his face had turned dark red. With a strangled sob, she tried to pry loose the hand that held her. He slapped her across the face again and again, and then backhand. She tried to twist away, but she could not escape the stinging, numbing blows. Her dress tore across the right shoulder. He stopped slapping her; instead, he balled up his fist and hit her hard in the belly. As she bent over, he released her. He raised a booted foot, put it on her hip, and shoved, sending her sprawling on the floor.

She lay there, sobbing, afraid to move, expecting him to kick her at any instant. He did not. She heard the scuffling of his boots as he moved toward the door of the room. Then, silently, quickly, she sprang to her feet and toward the desk. She saw Ethan's back as he went through the doorway. She pulled open a desk drawer and lifted out a loaded revolver.

But Ethan was gone.

She didn't follow him. She knew she couldn't have shot him. She had been pressed to the point where she could wish for his death, where she would have welcomed it; but to aim a gun at the back of Ethan's head and pull the trigger was quite a different thing.

Instead, she sank down into her chair at the desk once again. She lowered her forehead down onto her left hand. And, her right hand still on the pistol, she wept.

In time, her tears slowed and ceased, and then she might have dozed. As always after these episodes with Ethan, she was exhausted, and she felt that nothing would ever change, that she had always been in this hell and would never leave it. There had been a time when she blamed herself. An incident that had occurred with that black boy, Tracy, and Ethan had been suspicious of her ever since. She had never been able to allay those suspicions, and that had been her fault. . . . She no longer believed that. Now it seemed to her that Ethan would in-evitably have found a reason to suspect her and hate her and hurt her; it was in his nature. She wondered if it were in her nature to be a victim.

Something aroused her, some sound.

She sighed. She felt a little better now, relieved of her tears.

She heard the sound again—a footstep—and she looked up. With a small shock, she saw that a black was standing in the doorway looking at her. He shouldn't have been there; he had no business being in the house. Quickly she pulled her dress up over her right breast and lifted the pistol from the desk.

"Hannah—Miss Hannah—Mrs. Flynn," the black man said.

"What do you want?" His face was known to her, but she couldn't place him among the slaves of the plantation.

"I've got to talk to you—please. You *are* Hannah? Mi—Miz Hannah?"

"Of course, I'm Miz Hannah," she said sharply, and she pointed the gun directly at the man. "What's the matter with you?"

"Ma'am—please—you don't need that gun. My God, you must know me!"

The man didn't speak like a slave, and his accent wasn't entirely Deep South. He might have come from some-where farther north on the Delta, sold south perhaps, but . . .

She let the gun swing down toward the floor, almost dropping it, and a feeling of unreality swept over her. She stared at the black man.

"Oh, Jesus God," she murmured. "Tracy . . ."

From the moment they arrived at the plantation, his one thought was to get to Hannah. It didn't matter how weary he was, he had to reach her, and the sooner the better. If he had any hope at all of getting help from some-one, it was from her.

He didn't dare say anything about it to Barclay. Bar-clay, now overseer, appeared to take a vicious pleasure in

140

seeing him back again, and he looked at Alexandria with unconcealed lust. He led them to the cottage that Simon had occupied, telling them it was the only quarters available. "Ain't got no butler no more," he said, "and nobody hardly used this since you killed that black bastard."

Most of the hands were at work, and there was little recognition between Tracy and those few who saw him. Here and there a slave turned and stared, but he was too weary to stare back. He would look for old friends later.

Barclay took them to the supply shed, where they drew blankets and clothes. He told them they would be allowed one full day's rest, and then they were expected in the fields. "Don't you think you gon' get off easy 'cause you was a house nigger and a stable boy," Barclay said with satisfaction. "We ain't got much house help no more, and you ain't needed in the stables. Mr. Flynn say you both gon' into the fields, and by God, that just where you both gon'. . . ."

They washed at a pump and went into the cottage. It was hot and dirty, but they fell onto the bed with a vast feeling of relief. Then Tracy reminded himself that he must not rest, he must first of all look for Hannah.

Reaching her was easy, far easier than he had anticipated. Nobody stopped him as he walked to the back door of the mansion. He knocked and called out, but nobody answered. After a few minutes, he entered the house.

It seemed barren somehow; unlived in. There were no sounds of life, and the rooms and hallways had an empty feeling. He called out "Miss—Mrs. Hannah," for lack of anything better, and still received no answer. He knew he could be whipped or worse for being here, but surely Hannah wouldn't let anything like that happen if she could help it. And he had to find her.

There was no one, not even a maid. The house seemed to be completely empty, deserted. For no particular reason that he knew of, he entered the west wing. He had forgotten that it contained an office.

He looked through the doorway and saw the woman, her head down on the desk.

When she looked at him, he didn't recognize her at first,

though he spoke her name. She was pulling her torn dress up over one breast, and she was pointing a revolver at him. And then he saw that this *was* Hannah, a much older and taller Hannah, her face red and swollen and tear-stained, but my God, didn't she recognize him?

"Oh, Jesus God," she said. "Tracy . . ."

And then he was trying to tell her, trying to explain. . . .

Alexandria plodded across the fields toward the Flynn mansion. There was some semblance of a path, just as the overseer had told her, and by watching carefully, she could follow it. "Go to see Mr. Flynn," the overseer had said. "He sent word he want to see you right away."

Until now, she thought, she had always been lucky. She would never have chosen to be a white man's mistress if there had been any real alternative, but she could have lived a far worse life than the one which had been granted to her. She had learned to use the brains God had given her. She had been sold into a cathouse, but she had escaped the life of a field hand. The fields were hell, she knew that, and they might have killed her by this time.

Maybe they would yet.

Through the trees she saw the Flynn mansion, glistening white in the failing sunlight of late afternoon, and she paused. The day was still hot, and the dust stung her nostrils; she thought her lungs would never stop aching. She supposed she knew what Ethan Flynn wanted; he wanted to prove, finally, that no man, black or white, could take from him a woman he desired. She had spent only a few hours in his presence, but she felt she knew him better than she knew Tracy; while Tracy was different from anyone else she had ever met, she knew Ethan Flynn as a type. And this type was one she had always tried to avoid at all costs. She hoped he would be fast and that he wouldn't hurt her too much.

She forced herself forward. The big clumsy work shoes on her feet seemed to weigh tons and each step was an agony. Head down, she made her way through the trees and across the yard, hardly daring to pause again for fear she wouldn't be able to force herself any farther.

She struck the back door with her fist, and it opened

immediately. A young black woman wearing a flowered dress so wet it clung to her body looked out, then shouted back into the house, "She here, Mr. Ethan!"

"Well, bring her in, Jacintha," Alexandria heard him shout back, "bring her in!"

The sickness in the pit of Alexandria's stomach, a fearful anticipation of what was to come, worsened as she followed Jacintha through the doorway and into a large kitchen. But the scene there was quite unexpected. In the middle of the floor was a great oval-shaped tub with a high back, and in the tub sat Ethan Flynn. A second black girl, naked except for a red bandanna on her head, was dipping water out of the tub with a pitcher and pouring it over Ethan's head.

Alexandria hardly noticed Ethan or the two girls. She noticed nothing else about the kitchen at all. She was not surprised or shocked by the scene, unexpected though it was—a few weeks before, she might have been one of the girls, helping bathe her master or one of his guests. But now, her fear momentarily forgotten, she looked at that big tub of water and longed for one of her own as she had never before in her life longed for anything, anything at all. . . .

Jacintha poured a pitcher of water over Ethan, and he sputtered and laughed. Then: "Welcome home, Alexandria," he said.

"Yes, Mr. Flynn," she said dully.

"You gon' like it here."

"Yes, sir."

Ethan reached up and slapped the naked girl on the thigh. "Jacintha and Melonia here, they like it. Don't you girls?"

The two girls laughed, perhaps a little hollowly. Alexandria recognized their kind; they could be found anywhere, among whites as well as among blacks. She certainly didn't consider herself their superior; she had been one of them.

"Did Mr. Barclay show you where you and Tracy gon' stay?"

"Yes, sir."

"Nice little cottage, used to belong to a nigger man

Tracy killed. Least, so I heard tell. So I guess maybe Tracy deserves the place. Course it needs a mite fixing up, but I guess you and Tracy can take care of that, can't you?"

"Yes, sir." She was puzzled. This was not the kind of talk or behavior she had expected from Ethan Flynn, and she waited to see what he was driving at.

"I hope you understand, Alexandria, that you don't have to stay with Tracy if you don't want. I mean, honey, if you want more comfortable living—"

"I stay with him," she said quickly.

"Fine, fine—"

"He's my master." She said the words without thinking, a touch of defiance in her tone.

Ethan Flynn gave her a quick smile. "Course he's your master, if you say so, but I'm *his* master. I want to take you away from him, I do it. I want to give you to another nigger buck, I do that. I want you for myself, I simply take you. Hell, I can take you right now, if I want."

With that he stood up in the tub, water streaming down his big white body, and she involuntarily stepped back from him. He didn't appear to notice. The girl called Jacintha handed him a towel, and the one called Melonia began toweling his back.

"But I'm not gon' do anything like that, Alexandria," Ethan Flynn went on, stepping out of the tub. "Why should I? What would be the point? I *care* too much about you and Tracy to do a thing like that. I've known from the moment Tracy won you that you preferred to be with him, so I'm gon' let you stay with him. You can eat with him, sleep with him, work in the fields same as he does. You done chose to be with him, so you can share his life. *His* life, not mine. Do you understand me?"

"Yes, sir." And she did; she was beginning to understand what he was trying to do.

"Good. Just you remember you don't *have* to stay with him, Alexandria. You don't have to live with him, you don't have to work in the fields with him. Anytime you tire of that life, you can come here." He smiled at her. "That is, you can come here if you don't wait too long. I'm not a man who likes to be kept waiting."

"Yes, sir."

He looked at her in a way that told her he was seeing her as she had been on the night they had first met. But he showed no particular sign of desire. He stood before her, as indifferent to his own nakedness as she had been to hers, arrogant and unashamed. He would be arrogant with any woman, and she was just a black girl, a wench to be won or lost on the turn of a card, so why should he be ashamed?

"You're a beautiful girl, Alexandria," he said.

She looked at the floor without answering.

"I think you gon' want to stay beautiful long as you can." When she didn't answer, he said, "You can go now," as if he were tired of talking to her. "Go back to Tracy. See how you like the life of a field hand, you hear me?"

"Yes, sir."

"Go!"

He turned away from her and threw an arm around Melonia. He dropped his towel and reached for Jacintha. Alexandria, hardly daring to believe in her reprieve, left the kitchen and went back out into the hot afternoon. Behind her, she heard the laughter of Ethan Flynn and his black girls.

They sat facing each other in the dim afternoon light of the office, looking at each other with a kind of awe. This is Hannah, he kept telling himself, eleven years older and far different from anything he would have expected, yet undeniably still Hannah. Far different and yet—the ragged hair, the torn dress, the sunburned face and limbs—almost too much the same.

"I never understood clearly what happened," she told him. "I remember Simon went crazy, and I guess he dang near killed me. Someone said you killed him, but I didn't see that. My ole daddy, he packed me off to Europe, you may remember, along with my Aunt Rachel, and she wouldn't tell me nothing. And it was more'n four years before she died off and I came back. I heard something about you being sent to the Tennessee plantation, and I do remember daddy saying something about you being set free. Anyway, a little while after I got back, I up and married Ethan like I guess everybody expected, and then my ole daddy died off, and . . . well, here I am. . . ."

"Your daddy sent me to the Tennessee plantation to be freed," he told her. "Even though I'd saved your life—and I did, Miz Hannah—he thought best to free me on the sly. Some people wouldn't have approved, no matter what I'd done. Not Mr. Ethan, for instance, and not old Jonas Todd, your daddy's lawyer—"

"Oh, I believe you," she said, "and if it was up to me, I'd just give you a new manumission right now and let you go. But you've got to understand, I can't do that—"

"I do understand—"

"Only Ethan could do such a thing. I'm his wife. And that means he owns me just as much as he owns you. In fact, he owns me more, because you're legally free. So which one of us is really a slave?"

The deep fatigue of the journey began miraculously to fade, and before long, the mere fact of talking to Hannah seemed almost as important as what was said. She was unhappy, he saw; she had been weeping before he had entered the room, and her face was puffy as if she had been brutally slapped. From time to time she laughed, and her laughter was uncertain, as if she were learning how to do it all over again.

"I'll write to the Tennessee plantation," she told him. "There's got to be a record there that you were set free, and that'll be evidence. All we need is some evidence that my daddy let you go."

"Don't forget my company," he said. "They'll stand up for me."

Hannah looked doubtful. "But all they have is your word for it that you're free."

"Please write to them. Write to anyone who may be able to help."

"Oh, I will. But, of course, if Cousin Fayette has your original freedom paper, she'll be able to get you free fast as anybody else."

Yes, but he hadn't heard from Fayette in years, and apparently Hannah hadn't either. Since he had always felt that he could depend upon her, he didn't want to overlook

146

any possibilities. Hannah promised she would not only write the letters, she would look through her father's personal records for evidence of Tracy's freedom.

"Getting your woman free is gon' be a mite more difficult," she said.

"Alexandria's not really my woman," Tracy said. "I won her all right, but she knows that, as far as I'm concerned, the door is always open."

"You got no woman nowhere?"

"Nowhere."

She grinned at him suddenly. "You don't talk like your ole self no more, Tracy. You sound almost like a goddam Yankee."

"Give me a little time."

"You shoulda heard me talk when I come back from Europe. La-de-da!"

They both laughed, then smiled at each other, and Tracy leaned forward, his elbows on his knees.

"Are you happy, Miz Hannah?"

Her smile faded, and her eyes left his. "Well, you know . . . I guess you'll find out Ethan stays up at his house, and I came back here to my own four, five years ago. I guess that tells you something. Then Ethan took Wills' contract away from him and gave it to that damn peckerhead Barclay. I try to run this place the way my daddy woulda liked, but it ain't easy. I don't know. I get by. . . ."

"Remember when we were pickaninnies?" he asked.

"Oh, Christ," she said softly, and she smiled again. "Do I remember. . . ."

Remember when . . . remember when . . .

The afternoon passed and the room darkened. Neither of them thought to light a lamp.

"I suppose I'd better go before Mr. Ethan finds me here," Tracy said at last.

"No hurry. He don't even look in the door once a month. You want to stay out of his way, this is the best place you could be."

He stood up. "I'll remember that. But Alexandria is alone, and all this is new to her. She'll be frightened."

"Well . . . maybe we'll find a chance to talk again tomorrow."

"Fine."

When she stood up, her right breast slipped out of her torn dress. She said, "Oops!" and covered it again, adding with a grin, "Gon' lose a goddam boob! Not that you care much—you seen me grow 'em."

"Hell, Miz Hannah," he said, "I practically *helped* you grow 'em!"

They both laughed as they always had at their private jokes, inclining their heads toward each other, and she took a step toward him. They stood close together. She crossed her arms and cradled her breasts, holding her dress closed, and her nipples showed plainly through the thin cloth. Suddenly, in spite of his deep fatigue, he was terribly aware of her physical presence; and instinctively, he knew that she was just as aware of his.

"I guess this must be the last place in the world you want to be, Tracy," she said after a moment, "but I am so damn glad to see you, you don't know."

"And I'm glad to see you, too, Miz Hannah."

"How come you calling me Miz Hannah?"

"You know I've got to."

"Not when we're alone, you don't. You and me? It don't seem right."

He didn't trust himself to say anything more. His judgment was gone. He had been through too much, he was too tired, he needed rest. He suspected that the same thing was true of Hannah. So he said, "Maybe we can talk about that tomorrow."

She smiled at him and said, "Tomorrow."

To his surprise, Alexandria had done a great deal to make the cottage habitable. He had no idea where she had got the energy.

"Seen your lady friend, I guess," she said.

"I saw her."

"She gon' help you?"

"She's going to try. Don't you worry, Alexandria, we'll get away from here. Both of us."

"Funny place," Alexandria mused. "Him up at his house, her at her own."

148

"You've found out about that already."

She nodded. "That Mr. Barclay son-of-a-bitch, he say Mr. Ethan wants me to see him right away. I figured I knew what he wanted—what he didn't get on the *Duchess of Cairo*. But I was wrong. Or least he wasn't going to force me. Said I could stay with you or stay with him, as I pleased. Long as I didn't take too long to make up my mind."

"And you said?"

She shrugged. "Here I am, master man."

He laughed and kissed her on the top of her head, but she didn't smile.

"Sugar," she said after a moment, "are you scared of Mr. Ethan?"

"I was once. I don't think I am now."

"Well, you better be. Because he ain't like other men."

Something in her tone caught his attention. "How is Mr. Ethan different?" he asked.

"He ain't got no reason to go on living. That is, he ain't got no reason except one, and that is to do something bad. To hurt somebody or make somebody feel bad. That's why he likes fights where there's blood. Why he has women. Not to pleasure them for real, just to make them feel bad. That's why he got a wife, to make her feel bad. If he can't make somebody feel bad, he don't know what to do with hisself. He feels all tired and bored, and he'd just as soon be dead. And this makes him a very dangerous man, sugar. You fight with him, and he has one idea—to hurt you and maybe kill you or die hisself. He *wants* to die! I know this kind of man, sugar, and they only live to see how bad they can treat you before you turn 'round and kill them off."

Tracy wondered if she were right about Ethan. He didn't dispute that there were such men as Alexandria described, and Ethan might very well be one of them.

"Well, if worse comes to worse," he said, "we may just have to oblige friend Ethan. Or maybe his wife will."

Alexandria looked at him questioningly.

"She has a revolver," he said. "She keeps it in the middle drawer of a big oak desk in her office, and the office is

149

in the west wing of the house. If I had to, I could walk right to it this minute."

"How do you know—"

"I saw her put it there. And it's loaded."

chapter three

He thought of the pistol often, but he knew that to shoot Ethan would be an act of despair. Having killed the man, he would have very little chance of escaping. He would die for his act, and his only consolation would be the knowledge that Ethan was dead, too. But Ethan's death meant very little to Tracy, while his own life meant a great deal.

Tracy pondered the possibility of making an escape without killing Ethan. Escapes did occur, but there was very little chance that Alexandria and he could make a successful one together. Then separately? The odds would be very much against them, and besides, Tracy would have felt guilty about separating from the girl. To do so would be, in effect, abandoning her to her own fate, and he had come to feel responsible for her.

Escape, then, was a last resort. For the time being, he and Alexandria had to wait patiently for Hannah to receive replies to her letters or to turn up something useful in her father's records.

But when they went into the fields, it was easier to contemplate the pistol than to wait patiently. On their second full day on the plantation, they were taken to the fields for the first time in their lives.

They were awakened before dawn by a driver pounding on the door of their cottage. Tracy remembered enough of plantation life to get Alexandria to the cookhouse quickly —otherwise they would have no breakfast, since they were not prepared to cook their own. Under a shed roof, they hastily ate mush flavored with hog fat, salt, sugar, and a dash of milk. It wasn't a bad breakfast as slave fare went, better cooked and more savory than the food they'd had in the New Orleans slave jail, but Alexandria grumbled, "God, sugar, I still can't believe there's people that *live* on this shit."

They were finishing the mush when the others started falling into work gangs. Tracy remembered that when he was a boy, spirits at this time of the day had been fairly good, particularly among the younger blacks, and there had been a certain amount of joking and laughing. There was very little now.

A driver carrying a whip approached them. Tracy couldn't be sure, but he thought the driver was Bardo. "You get your ass over to *that* gang," he said to Tracy, pointing; and to Alexandria, "And you haul your pretty little butt over there—"

"Let her stay with me," Tracy said quickly. But then he suddenly remembered that husbands and wives, men and their women, were always put into different gangs.

"Don't just stand there," the driver said. "Move!"

"Please, Bardo—"

Completely without warning, the driver swung the heavy butt of his whip and caught Tracy across the face. His cheek bone and nose seemed to explode, and he went blind. When his sight began to clear, he found himself on his hands and knees without knowing how he got there. Something warm and wet dripped onto the backs of his hands, and he was surprised to see that it was blood.

"You got the wrong name, boy," the driver said. "I'se Varden, and don't you forget it. The master say you a troublemaker. Well, you ain't gon' make no trouble, you hear me?"

Tracy struggled to his feet. Fortunately, the struggle

was a long one, because the strength of anger was coming to him, and his first thought was simply to kill the man who had hit him. Then he found Alexandria in front of him, and he realized that she was frightened that he would do just that.

"You hear me, boy?" the driver repeated.

Tracy managed to nod.

"Then move, both you."

Alexandria reluctantly left for her gang. Tracy gave the driver a final look and walked toward his. Somebody laughed and said, "First blood of the day."

Not all the slaves worked in gangs. Cooks, blacksmiths, cobblers, seamstresses, and others had specific tasks, which they might perform as they pleased, as long as the work was done by the time it was needed. These stood by and watched as the field hands picked up their hoes and rakes and other tools. The sun was just beginning to come up, a hot pink that would soon be a molten white.

The drivers swiftly moved the gangs into the fields. They were generally the bigger, stronger men with a taste for power and a knack for policing. They might have been troublemakers themselves if they hadn't been drivers, but their violence was channeled. Their philosophy was: "If it's gon' be your ass or mine, it sure hell ain't gon' be mine."

Tracy was in a gang of about twenty. They fanned out and began moving across a field at a slow pace. Tracy had a hoe in his hand, and he found that he didn't really know what to do with it. He looked around to see what the others were doing.

"You!" said the driver, pointing at him with the butt of his whip. "You! Bend over that hoe."

Tracy tried to explain. "I'm just trying to understand what I'm supposed—"

"Bend over that hoe, I say!" The driver was hurrying toward him. "Don't you shirk on me, boy!"

"I'm not shirking, I just want—"

The whip cut him off. It shot out too fast to be seen and cut across Tracy's shoulder like a bullet. He gasped with pain.

"Bend over that hoe! Make that hoe move!" The whip

shot out again, this time cutting across both shoulders. "I won't tell you no more. You move with the others, and you don't miss no weed, no nothing. You shirk on me, I gon' whip you dead!"

Tracy bent over his hoe and tried to imitate the movements of the others in the gang. He now knew that he was supposed to pull or kill weeds. He would do that, or at least try.

The driver, of course, now had his eye on Tracy. Time and again, he came over and inspected the rows Tracy was weeding, found weeds that had been missed, and made Tracy go back and pull them up. The man seemed impossible to satisfy, but Tracy did as he was told and did it quickly.

By the time the sun was well up, his soft gambler's hands had begun to blister. He tried to grip the hoe to minimize the blistering, but it quickly became worse. Long before noon he paused to look at palms and fingers that were raw almost to the point of bleeding.

"You! You shirking again?"

"No, I'm not shirking—"

"You grab that hoe!"

"My hands—"

The whip cracked across Tracy's back, making him wrench with pain, and once again, for a blind instant, he was in danger of attacking. Somehow he restrained himself. Resistance could only take him to the post, where he would get far worse than he was getting now. He grabbed at the hoe with stinging hands and chopped away at the earth.

"You don't let me see you drop that hoe again, boy! I say I gon' lash you dead, I mean it!"

There was little talk between the field hands. A word or two was allowed now and then, but when the chatter continued for too long, Tracy saw the whip land on someone other than himself. Singing was permitted, and from time to time, someone would start a verse and soon be joined by a few others. The rhythms of the songs helped the work, somehow lightening it.

Twice during the morning a boy came by with a communal bucket of water, and each hand was allowed a sip.

Tracy was drenched with sweat; the little water he was given hardly seemed adequate, but he knew that more might make him ill. He remembered the old trick of placing a pebble under the tongue to help relieve the mouth's dryness.

Shortly after noon, lunch was brought to the hands in the field. On the first day, it consisted of corn biscuits and water, and even the driver complained loudly of its inadequacy. They ate in a small grove, and afterwards, the men and women were allowed to go to opposite sides to relieve themselves on the edge of the fields. There followed a short rest period, and a slave who claimed to remember Tracy examined his hands. "You be all right," he said. "The hoe hurt'em and the hoe heal'em. Four, five days, your hands be most as hard as mine."

In the afternoon, Varden rode up on a mule. He stared at Tracy, who pretended not to notice but kept right on working. Tracy was learning.

"Your new one giving you any trouble?" Varden asked the driver.

"Don't no one never give me trouble."

Varden laughed and rode off.

The afternoon was far worse than the morning. The glaring sunlight and the sweat that ran into Tracy's eyes blinded him. The muscles of his arms and legs ached, and his back seemed on the verge of breaking. His hands were like fire, and he could barely move his fingers and grip his hoe. He faltered, and the whip came down on him again. The slave who had examined Tracy's hands objected on his behalf and got the whip himself for his trouble. There was a short rest period in the middle of the afternoon, but the remainder of the workday was pure nightmare. Through a haze of pain, Tracy was aware of swinging his hoe, of its *chuck*ing sound, of pulling it free of the earth, of very little else.

The fields were hell.

And he would be back here again tomorrow.

And the next day and the next and the next . . . he would always be here, here in hell, time without end. . . .

And then, miraculously, the sun was dropping rapidly toward the horizon, and the gangs were leaving the fields.

Tracy was almost too tired to appreciate the miracle. Like a drunk, he found himself with gaps in his consciousness: he was suddenly at the pump in the yard of Simon's cottage (to him it would always be Simon's cottage), tearing off all of his clothes in the dusk, heedless of who might see him. Alexandria pumped water over him and worried about his whip-marks, and then he worked the pump handle for her. She had been whipped only a couple of times, she said, and not very hard, but her hands were as raw as Tracy's. When they were through at the pump, he picked up his clothes and went into the cottage while she went off to the cookhouse to get food for them.

Their supper was by far the best meal of the day—boiled greens, a piece of smoked ham, more corn biscuits—but they were too tired to appreciate it. They scarcely talked. When they were through eating, Tracy immediately climbed into bed, and a few minutes later, Alexandria pulled off her dress and joined him.

She adjusted the mosquito bar, then sat beside him, staring at her hands, her naked figure barely discernible in the hot dark.

"It's going to be all right," he said, taking her hands in his.

She didn't answer. She lay down with her head on his shoulder, and he suppressed a groan: he was far too weary for such closeness, for the sticky heat of her body and the weight of her head. She toyed with him, but he didn't respond. He didn't want to respond; for the first time in his life, he felt far too desperately tired, cheated of the consolations of the flesh by fatigue, the burning sun, and the whip. Still, when she brought his hand to her tenderest flesh, he tried to please her.

But almost immediately, he realized that she was sound asleep.

And then . . .

There was a pounding on the door.

The sun was coming up, and it was time to return to hell.

"Things change fast after Mr. Add die and Mr. Ethan take over," Isaiah told him. Isaiah, badly crippled by the blow Simon had given him, still worked in the stables. "Life for a black man ain't never easy, but leastways Mr. Add weren't a mean man. Not most times. He always like to see his people get some good times as well as bad, and he try to take care of them. Give them good clothes, good food, good doctoring. He never sell no one that weren't mean and evil, and he never make his black wenches bed with him or let his overseer bed them."

Tracy saw that time had lent a certain enchantment to the past, but he would not have disagreed too drastically. He continued to listen.

"But Mr. Ethan's a lot different," Isaiah went on. "Mean. Wicked. Don't care for nothing. Mr. Add, he never allow no knife fighting, but Mr. Ethan, he like to get a lot of white masters in his barn, all wenching and drinking and wagering on anything, then he get a couple of niggers to cut each other up for some wench. That how ole Florian got hisself killed. Master say, 'Florian, you know that little wench you been wanting? You gone have her. But first you got to cut up that nigger right over there. And if'n you *don't* cut up that nigger right over there, I gon' give that wench to *him,* and by God, I gon' make you watch him take her.' So Florian fight, and the other nigger spill Florian's guts. Slice him right up the middle. Other nigger so sick he can't take the wench. Hell, he don't want to kill nobody.

"Mr. Ethan, all he care about, he lose a good twelve-hundred-dollar nigger. He take the wench for himself. He take *any* wench he want any time. And he don't care if Mr. Barclay or Mr. Enright do the same. Mr. Wills never touch no black wench, but Mr. Barclay got anyway six black pickaninnies running around 'sides his own seven white ones. And he always sniffing up Miz Hannah's ass till she sass him off and say she gon' cut him up. That lady get going, she got a tongue like a goddam bullwhip.

"Miz Hannah, she tough. Not mean like Mr. Ethan, not kind like her ole daddy, just plain ole tough as a leather titty, and I guess she got to be, married to Mr. Ethan.

"Yes, times is changed. Lots of folks you knowed is dead or sold away, the day is longer and the work is harder, and Saturday night ain't so much fun anymore. . . .

Long time ago, I hear tell that after you went to Tennessee, Mr. Add set you free. But nobody here know for sure it's true. Guess now it weren't. . . ."

The second day in the fields was, if anything, worse than the first. The blistering hands, the heat of the sun, the blow of the whip, all seemed meant to grind him down, to reduce him to something less than himself. By afternoon, he could hardly raise his head, and that night, he and Alexandria fell into bed more exhausted than ever.

The third day was as bad as the second, but it turned out to be a Saturday—Tracy had lost track of the days—and they left the fields an hour early. Isaiah was right, however: Saturday night was not the fun that Tracy remembered. Not that that mattered to him; he and Alexandria were conscious only of their captivity.

I am no slave, he reminded himself as he lay in bed that night, *I am no slave. I am a free man, and I shall be free. I shall be free.*

But now it seemed to him that the nightmare was reality and that he was giving voice to a dream.

The next morning Alexandria was assigned to the cookhouse. When she was allowed to leave shortly after noon, Tracy took her to the stream where the Sunday bathing had taken place when he was a boy. There were not nearly as many people there as he remembered, and there was no more sense of joy or release than there had been on Saturday night.

"I want to show you something," he told Alexandria.

After eleven years, he still felt the rise of fear and a slight racing of his heart as he walked Alexandria along the bank of the river toward the place where he and Hannah had encountered Ethan and his friends. He had told her very little of what had happened; the story had always stuck in his throat. Now, as they walked along, he forced himself to tell her in detail. It was as if he were trying somehow to connect the past to his present circumstances and at the same time rid himself of the past.

When they reached the place in the stream where he and Hannah had reentered the water, he peered almost fearfully at the woods on the opposite bank; he could easily believe that Ethan, the Colby boys, Follett, and two others might appear at any instant. He sat on the bank with Alexandria and without looking at her he told her everything that happened up to the moment Simon rescued him. He then told how he was whipped. The rest of the story could wait for another time.

"Well, sugar," Alexandria murmured a long moment after he had stopped speaking, "you're still alive and you're still all man. And I can prove it. Let's go in the water."

They stripped, and Tracy followed Alexandria into the stream. The water, almost as cold as he remembered it, felt good, and for the first time since their arrival, a kind of physical relief swept over him. But he still felt haunted, as if at any instant he might look up and see Ethan standing on the bank, grinning down at them, a knife in his hand.

Alexandria seemed to know instinctively what troubled him. When they had played in the water for a little while, she slid an arm over his shoulder, kissed him, fondled him.

"Ain't no Mr. Ethan here now," she said as he came alive for the first time in days, "ain't gon' to be no Mr. Ethan here. Nobody here but just us, just you and me."

No, no one was there but the two of them. And as they drew together, no one interrupted them. There were, at last, a few hours of bliss and forgetfulness. But when the sun began to lower and they left the stream, Tracy realized that he still had not rid himself of the past. He looked at the patch of woods, sleepy and deserted in the late afternoon, and there was still fear among the trees. Sweet things had happened in this stream eleven years ago, and terrible things had happened among the trees, and none of those things was finished. Ethan Flynn would not let them be finished. Not yet.

And the next day was hell again.

And the next and the next and the next, until one was quite indistinguishable from another.

They were blacks, slaves, her inferiors; she had come to accept that without ever giving the matter much thought. It was conveyed to her by the time and place and circumstances. She didn't hate the blacks, as Ethan frequently seemed to do, nor did she spend much pity on them. She was their mistress, they did as she ordered, she owned them; therefore she was their superior. She would have felt precisely the same if they had been white.

Tracy was quite a different matter. She had had a special relationship with him from the time they were infants. Ordinarily that relationship would have died and been replaced by a vague sentimental memory, but she found now that it never had. She had been too closely bound to him, and even Ethan, with his repeated reminders and accusations, had contributed to keeping the relationship alive. Hence his blackness and her whiteness, his slavery and her freedom, were irrelevant. He was a man, and she was a woman.

Each evening she waited for him after the hands had returned from the fields. The first few evenings, when he didn't appear, she told herself that she wasn't disappointed and that she hadn't really expected him. After all, Tracy was unused to field work and would be terribly tired, and besides he would know that it was too soon for answers to the letters she had written.

On Tuesday evening, a week after his arrival, he came to her office, and they sat together in the dark for more than an hour, talking about old times. She told him that none of her few house blacks stayed with her and that whenever he wanted to see her in the evening, he had only to slip discreetly through the door. . . .

He visited her again on Thursday evening.

As soon as he had left, she went upstairs to bed. Neither of them had mentioned the day that Ethan had caught them together, but as she lay in the dark, she meticulously reconstructed everything that had happened up until the moment when Ethan and the others had appeared. And then she tried to envision what might have happened if only they had been left alone. . . .

On Friday and Saturday, she saw nothing of Tracy. When he failed to appear on Sunday afternoon, she went looking for him but didn't find him. He was not among the blacks who went bathing in the stream. It occurred to her that he might have gone upstream to that pool where they had been alone together, but some instinct made her stay away.

He came to her office again the next evening.

After that she no longer tried to hide from herself her bitter disappointment when he didn't appear. It was that damned Alexandria who was keeping him away, she told herself. Little black bitch! They were living together in that cottage, and she knew perfectly well they weren't spending their nights holding hands. They didn't have to stay together—either of them could have found a place in the bunkhouse if they'd wanted to. Or Tracy could have stayed right here in the house—she quickly cut off that line of thought. But no, when you got right down to it, that goddam Tracy was just like Ethan and Barclay and all other men. Peckerheads, all of them! All any of them ever really gave a damn about was tail, tail, tail, and right at this very moment, Tracy and that Alexandria wench were probably naked and stewing in bed. . . .

She pounded her desk top in frustration.

Soon after Tracy's arrival, Hannah paid a visit to Ethan, something she avoided doing as much as possible. She found him supervising the stacking of wood in the sugar house of the Flynn plantation.

"Why didn't you tell me Tracy was one of the slaves you brought back?" she asked him.

"You knew the coffle had left two slaves with you—how was I to know you didn't know who they were? Besides, the way you lit into me the minute I stuck my head in the door, it didn't seem to matter if you knew or not. You'd find out sooner or later. Make a nice surprise for you."

"Ethan, Tracy Carter is a free man."

Ethan grinned at her—the cocky, self-assured, boyish grin he had never lost and never would until he died. "The hell you say, honey. I paid for him, and anything I paid for is mine."

"But you must know he's free—you met him as a free man—"

"He told you all about it, did he? For all I know he was a runaway."

"But my father told me—"

"I don't give a damn what your old daddy told you. He's dead, and I'm not."

She saw that there was no point in arguing the matter with him; she hadn't really thought there would be. She had come here with something else in mind.

"Barclay told me you give him strict orders both Tracy and his wench were to work in the fields."

"That's right."

She tried to strike a reasonable note. "But they ain't field hands, Ethan, specially that Alexandria. I can use her in the cookhouse. And Isaiah can surely use Tracy in the stables—"

"They stay in the fields."

"But why—"

"I'm going to toughen Tracy up, make a knifer out of him."

Hannah stared at Ethan for a long moment. "Get him all cut up, you mean. Get him all slashed and scarred and finally killed. That's what you have in mind for Tracy, isn't it?"

Ethan shrugged and smiled.

"And Alexandria?" Hannah asked. "Why you want to keep her in the fields?"

"Soften her up. Toughen up Tracy and soften Alexandria."

"Whyn't you just rape her?"

"This is more interesting."

Hannah shook her head slowly and wonderingly. "You're truly filth, aren't you? As bad as anything in a New Orleans back alley—"

"Listen!" Ethan suddenly wheeled on her and seized her face with one hand, his palm cupping her chin and his fingers and thumb digging painfully into her cheeks. Her eyes widened with fear in spite of herself.

"Do you know what we sometimes do to give nigger knife-fighters incentive?" he continued in a low tense voice. "We give them a nice juicy little wench to fight over, winner gets to stud her, and like as not we all stand 'round and watch. You know that, don't you?"

"Yes!"

162

"Well, one of these days that's what I'm going to use you for. And you're going to love it, because that's the kind of filth *you* are. Nothing you'd like better than having a nigger, still bloody and hot from the battle, ramming it up you——"

She tore away from him and ran, and behind her, she heard his laughter.

The first answer to the letters she had written came from the Tennessee plantation. She could have taken it to the cottage to show Tracy, but she didn't. She waited two days for him to come to her, because she wanted to be alone with him when he read it.

"I'm sorry," she said, handing it to him.

Her words shook him visibly; he was even more shaken after he had read the letter. He leaned toward the lamp on her desk and rapidly went over the message a second time, as if he couldn't believe he had read it correctly the first.

"But it says I never was freed." He sounded stunned.

"I know. It says you were sold off——"

"But that's not true! You've got to believe me, your father did have me freed!"

"I do believe you."

"He's lying. Your overseer up there is lying."

"Course he is. Ethan probably told him long ago how to answer any questions about you. Probably told him to change all the records up there in Tennessee, just in case."

Tracy shook his head as if still dazed. "I suppose I should have expected this. I guess in a way I did. But now that it's actually happened. . . ."

"I know. But we'll find something, if not in my father's papers, then maybe in Mr. Jonas Todd's. If I can get permission——"

"No." Tracy shook his head. "If Mr. Ethan has bothered to change one set of records, he'll have taken care of them all. I don't think you're going to find a thing."

"But we've got to try. And we still have to hear from your company, you know."

Tracy looked up hopefully. "Yes, they'll stand up for me. I'm just surprised you haven't heard from them yet."

"Don't you worry, we'll hear from them soon. But these things take time."

"Yes, of course. They wouldn't just ignore your letter." A note of desperation had entered his voice. "I'm too important to them, and this is too important to me."

"You absolutely right! They're probably doing something about it right now."

"I hope so."

But he sounded anything but hopeful, and he looked ill. He stood up slowly and said he was going back to the cottage; he was weary, he needed rest. She tried to persuade him to stay with her a little longer, but failed. He left.

And she was guilt-stricken because she was happy—happy that she hadn't yet lost him.

The sun was a white-hot pestle that ground down the blacks in the mortar of the fields. Now and then Tracy caught sight of Alexandria, and he watched her worriedly, hoping she would be all right. Every day he saw slaves crumple and fall, and during a single day, two men and a woman died. Hannah called Barclay a "murderous bastard" for overworking them, and Barclay swore he would "kill that bitch yet."

But not all the illness and death was in the fields. The hospital was overflowing with cases of malaria, yellow fever, flux, and a dozen other complaints. Sometimes Tracy heard the groans and whimpers of the ill in the middle of the night, though the cottage was a hundred yards from the hospital. Not one baby that had been born since Tracy's arrival on the plantation had survived.

The days and nights dragged on. Alexandria reported with weary indifference that she thought she was pregnant; later she reported just as indifferently that she was not. Tracy discovered that it was possible not to care one way or the other. Fatigue and growing despair were taking their toll.

One morning Tracy was told to report to the Flynn plantation. There he was conducted to the barn where Ethan Flynn was waiting for him.

"You gon' learn some knife fighting, boy," he announced.

Tracy replied in a carefully neutral voice, "I don't think I'd be very good at that."

"Then I guess you gon' get yourself cut up some. 'Cause you ain't got no choice," Ethan said, indicating two drivers with whips behind him.

Ethan stripped to the waist before him. He and Ethan each had a padded stick, and it was fight or be whipped. Nevertheless, he tried only to ward off Ethan's blows and refused to attack, and within a few minutes, Ethan gave up in disgust.

"Ah, shit!" He tossed his stick aside and picked up a wicked-looking knife. He took the knife to one of the drivers and traded it for the driver's whip. "I guess you gon' have to cut up this boy a little."

The driver grinned and accepted the knife. He moved around Tracy, watching him carefully, as if measuring him. Tracy felt as if he were growing hollow, and his mouth went dry. He raised his stick involuntarily, never daring to take his eyes off the other man.

The driver attacked.

Again, there was no real escape, but Tracy managed to dance to one side as his opponent slashed out at him. A second attack followed immediately; Tracy warded off a knife slash with his stick, but then tripped up on his own feet and fell. For a moment, he thought the driver was going to attack him where he lay, but then the man smiled, licked his lips, and backed off.

"Up," Ethan said, shaking his whip. "On your feet."

Tracy slowly regained his feet, his gaze never leaving the other man, fully conscious of the fact that he might die within the next few seconds.

The driver attacked again. This time he brandished the knife in a blindingly swift and complex pattern, and Tracy could do nothing to ward it off. Suddenly the blade was cutting down across him from his left shoulder to his waist, a numbing lightninglike blow, and Tracy heard himself roar with rage and terror. He drove his stick point-first into the other man's belly, all of his strength behind it, and the driver retched horribly. The next thing he knew, he was bringing the stick down across the man's wrist, and he heard the crack of the breaking bone and saw the knife drop. Then, as the man fell, he clubbed him across the back of the head as hard as he could.

The driver lay still. Tracy stood over him, panting, ready to strike again if necessary.

After a moment, Ethan laughed. "By God, I think we gon' make a fighter of you yet. But you didn't have to kill him, did you? Look at your chest."

Tracy looked. There was no cut and no blood. The knife had had no edge.

Tracy spent at least two hours of every morning undergoing training, and he put his heart into it. *Just you wait, Mr. Ethan,* he thought, *just you keep on teaching me. I'm a good pupil. And one of these days I'm going to put this knife into your chest. . . .*

He fell into the habit of seeing Hannah almost every evening if only for a few minutes, but there was never any news.

"Maybe your letter never reached my company—"

"I thought of that. Ethan might have got hold of it somehow, or more likely he could have got hold of the answer. So I wrote again. I'll write again and again, if I have to. And I wrote to your bank in Cincinnati, just in case they can help you. Tracy, I'll write to anyone you say. And if you want to write, I'll post the letters."

"I can't understand why we haven't heard from Fayette."

"I'll write to her again, too."

"If you get an answer, you won't wait to tell me, will you? You'll tell me right away?"

"Course I will! I won't even wait for you to come in from the fields. I'll bring it to you."

She kept her promise. On a burning afternoon, he saw her come plodding through the fields. As usual, she wore an ordinary straw hat and cotton dress and sandals, and she might have been taken for a female field hand, but he recognized her at once even at a distance. Alexandria happened to be in the next gang, and Tracy looked at her. He saw that she too had spotted Hannah. She paused at her work until the driver of her gang shook his whip at her. Tracy's heart thumped.

After a few minutes, Hannah reached the edge of the field that Tracy's gang was working, and his driver went to meet her. They spoke, and Hannah pointed at Tracy. The driver yelled, "Tracy, you get yourself over here! I mean run, nigger, run!"

Tracy forced himself to lope over to Hannah, and the driver left. Hannah was holding a piece of paper, a letter, in her hand, and he saw by her face that the news was bad. Without saying a word, he took the letter from her and read it.

"They're not going to help me," he said after a minute. "My own company. They say there's nothing they can do."

"I know."

"They say they like me, and they want me back." His words had a bitter taste and felt like acid in his throat. But he went on speaking, saying what Hannah already knew. "They say they have no evidence that I'm either free or slave. And they remind you that the burden of proof that I'm free is entirely on me. Because I'm black. Because I'm a nigger."

"Tracy, we still ain't heard from Cousin Fayette—"

"And we're not going to."

"Course we are! And I'm writing to other relatives who can put me in touch with her?"

"Why the hell bother?"

"She's the one who really counts, Tracy. This goddam company of yours don't count! Cousin Fayette can go right to some abolitionist lawyer up north and before long, Ethan will *have* to let you go!"

"Only it ain't gon' happen. Ain't you heard, Miz Hannah, Mr. Ethan, he got my ass, he gon' keep it—"

"Tracy, you stop that!"

"The rest was just a dream. Now I got a row to hoe, so get the hell out of my field."

He dropped the letter and ran back to his hoe. Something strange seemed to be happening inside of him, as if something were crumbling, and he thought of Simon during the last bad days of the majordomo's life. He picked up the hoe and began chopping away with it, and the sweat running into his eyes turned the world into a dream-like blur. He saw Hannah walking away, back toward the house.

His hoe caught on a tough weed, and he bellowed with anger as he pulled the blade free.

He lifted the hoe high and chopped eratically with all his strength.

"Boy, you watch what you doing!" the driver shouted.

Tracy lifted the hoe over his head and looked around to see if the driver were within range of a blow, and the others in the gang backed off from him.

Alexandria called, "Tracy!" and he looked around toward her. She was running toward him. As she passed the driver of her gang, he shot his whip out around her ankles and tripped her up. She sprawled headlong, and the driver quickly freed his whip and raised it over his head. He brought it down across her back, and she cried out. By that time, Tracy was running toward the driver.

Someone, he had no idea who, grabbed him. The hoe was pulled from his hands. Then he was free, but a whip cut across his shoulders. He grabbed the whip and pulled it away from the driver, the same driver who had been beating Alexandria. He slugged the man three times with the butt, knocking him down, then began whipping him. The howling driver tried to crawl away.

Then they had him again, his arms twisted behind him, and they were dragging him through the fields.

"You touch that girl, I'll kill you!" he screamed. "I swear to God! I'll kill you! I'll kill you!

"Seventy-five lashes in sets of twenty-five," Ethan said jovially, "and by God, this time we gon' do it right! Ain't that so, Tracy, boy? Mr. Barclay, you damn well better lay it on, 'cause if you don't, I'm gon' lay it on you. If he faints, you just dash water on him and wait till he comes to. I want that boy to get every last stripe, and then maybe we'll give him seventy-five more."

This time there was no one to take any part of the whipping for him. He was stripped naked, tied to the post, and before the blacks of two plantations, the whipping began.

And seemed to go on forever.

Before the seventy-fifth stripe, he was beyond humiliation. He knew only pain, pain that would continue for days. Barclay and Varden carried him to the cottage, flung him onto the bed, and left him in Alexandria's care.

And on his first day back in the fields, she left him. It was not a bad day, despite the fact that he was still too painfully stiff to work. His driver was almost gentle and didn't press him. The hands working closest to him gave him all the help they could. The water boy came to him frequently.

There was just one disturbing incident. It happened that Alexandria's gang was again working next to Tracy's, and she tried to keep watch on him to see that he was all right. Perhaps her driver thought she was shirking. Tracy had no idea if this were the same driver he had beaten or not, but he heard the man speak roughly to Alexandria and saw him raise his whip. Then the driver saw Tracy staring at him, and so did Alexandria. And in the silence of the next few seconds, there was a memory of Tracy's warning and his threat to kill.

The driver lowered his whip.

That evening after they had washed and eaten, Alexandria sat on the side of the bed where Tracy was lying face down in the dark. For a long time neither of them said a word.

Then she said, "Tracy, I'm gon' . . . Tracy, I am going to leave you."

Something within him wrenched, but he didn't answer.

"You'll let me leave you, won't you?"

"You know the door is always open."

"But if I walk through it, you'll close it."

Again he didn't answer.

"My goddam hands," she went on. "Every day they get more like the paws of some animal. What man wants hands like these touching him? I'm a whore, Tracy, not a field hand, and the fields are making me ugly. I'm not made for this life, nobody is, and I don't want to be old and ugly before my time. You can understand that, can't you?"

"I understand."

"Besides, you'll be better off without me. One of these days, you're going to see someone take a whip to me, and you're going to get yourself killed—"

"You don't have to leave on account of me."

"I know I don't."

He felt the bed move as she stood up and heard her footsteps as she walked to the door.

"I suppose I'd best leave right now," she said. "No need dragging this out. . . . Tracy?"

"Yes."

"All you got to do is say I *can't* go—"

"I don't own nobody."

He felt her presence in the darkness of the room for another minute. Then she said, "Thank you. I guess I'll always sort of love you." And she left him.

chapter four

"Goddam, man," Tracy said, laughing, "you take care with that whip—you gon' find it wrap around your own ass!"

Others in the gang laughed, and the driver grinned. "You want to try it?"

"Hell, yes. You work my row for me, and I promise to whip your ass for you."

There was more laughter, and the driver said, "All right, that enough, now. You all keep them hoes moving, or Varden'll be down on us."

Tracy immediately started a work song, and the others joined in with him. He still had some aches from the whipping, but he had never felt better in his life, and his good spirits were infectious. No other work gang had higher spirits than his, and no other did better work with less agony. The fields were still hell, but they were much less so when Tracy was nearby.

He was a puzzle to the others. They had recently seen him take a bad whipping, and they knew that even more recently his woman had left him, and yet he was as happy a man as you could find on the Carter and Flynn plantations. No one knew why, and Tracy passed the matter off with jokes.

The reason was simple. One evening, some days after Tracy had returned to the fields, a boy came to him with the message that Miz Hannah wanted to see him right away. Tracy hadn't spoken to her since the day of the whipping. When he reached her office, he found her smiling and excited.

"Tracy, I heard from Boston!"

"From Fayette?" He quite literally could not believe he was hearing correctly.

"No, but I know now why she ain't answered, and you can bet she'll answer yet! Tracy, up till now she ain't even got my letters, but when she gets them . . ."

Hannah reminded him that she had promised to write to other relatives in Boston. She had done so and had received a reply to the effect that Fayette had been abroad for quite some time and was expected home from England very soon. Meanwhile, her mail was being held in Boston, as that was the fastest and surest way of getting it to her. Yes, Cousin Hannah's letters had arrived safely, and Fayette's attention would be directed to them on the very day of her arrival. Tracy listened, stunned.

"So you see, she'll have my letters any day now. She may even be at home and have them right this minute. And the minute she reads them, she'll do something about it, you can count on it! You know what: I'm gon' write her another letter right now."

Tracy sank into a chair. He felt as if he were awakening from a bad dream.

"I figured it was best not to tell you about this in the fields," Hannah went on. "Best nobody but us has any idea that something important's happening."

Tracy nodded.

"I tell you something now, Tracy. Cousin Fayette always was your only hope. There weren't nothing your Cincinnati bank could do. Your company couldn't help you even if it wanted, and our Tennessee plantation weren't about to. From what you told me, Cousin Fayette was the only person in the whole wide world could do a thing."

"I know that," he said softly. "I always knew that. But I had to believe there was a whole wide world out there ready to help me. Only there wasn't."

"And now all we got to do is figure out how to get your woman free."

Tracy shook his head. "I've got to get her free, all right, but I told you—she's not my woman. Not really. And anyway, she left me."

Hannah looked at him sharply. "For Ethan," she said.

"Yes."

"Son of a bitch gets everything he wants, don't he?" she mused. "Me, you, that girl . . . Well, anyway he ain't gon' hang onto you. . . . Hey, we got to have a drink!"

On the desk were a jug, a pitcher of water, and a couple glasses, all evidently brought here for this occasion, and Hannah set about pouring two drinks. Tracy watched her, his elation growing every minute.

When she turned toward him, a glass in each hand, and smiled, her effect on him was suddenly very physical.

Once again, as on the day of his return to the Carter plantation, each was overwhelmingly aware of the other's physical presence. Hannah seemed to catch her breath and sway dizzily. Tracy looked at her dark nipples pressed against her dress and remembered seeing her bare breast on that first day. He looked at the shadow of her navel and the dark rise of her pubic mound and remembered the many times, eleven years ago and more, when he and she had played together. . . .

She padded across the room toward him on bare feet. He started to rise, but she motioned him not to. She went to his side, much closer than necessary, and handed him a glass.

"Thank you."

"You welcome. Here's to your freedom."

They drank, she still standing beside him. Her legs leaned against his thigh, and she put a forearm around his shoulders.

"I'm glad for you, Tracy," she said, "but being selfish, I'm gon' to be the sorriest woman in the world to see you go."

She swayed toward him slightly as she took another sip

from her glass, and her nearness was more intoxicating than the liquor. He brought an arm around her thighs and lightly cupped a buttock. She immediately brought a knee onto his lap and leaned forward and kissed him hard on the mouth. In that moment, he knew he could do anything he wished to her, or with her, anything at all.

But he did nothing, and the moment passed. She raised her head, smiling slightly, and shook it as if to clear it. She said, "That was nice," and slipped away from him.

She walked to her desk, dropped sprawling into a chair, and twisted to face him. He wondered if she realized that every movement she made was an invitation to him, an invitation and a challenge.

He finished his drink at a gulp.

"I think I'd better go now."

Her smile disappeared. "So soon? You only been here a few minutes."

"It's been a hard day, and I'm all shaken up by this news. Scared I'll do something or say something I shouldn't, if you want to know the truth—"

"You can do or say anything you please with me," she said quite innocently, shifting her thighs, "you know that."

He stood up. He dared accept no invitations or challenges now, dared love no one. To love meant an emotional involvement and a threat to his coming freedom. When he regained his freedom, he wanted to leave as little as possible behind. He could love only in freedom or in defeat.

He said, "I know, Hannah, but I must leave. Please forgive me."

"Only if you promise to spend the evening with me tomorrow," she said. "Anyway, I suppose you'll want to come here every evening to see if there's news from Boston."

"That's right, I will," he said, "and I promise."

He left the office.

The knife fighting sessions had been resumed, and Tracy knew his secret was most in danger during the two hours when he was with Ethan. Ethan was sharp-eyed, he was shrewd, and he quickly detected that some kind of change had occurred in Tracy. But he was puzzled by its nature.

"By God, boy, I think you truly getting to like that knife. How about that, now?"

"I just do what you tell me, Mr. Ethan."

"No, sir, I think you're getting a taste for steel. Maybe you're even getting some damn fool idea about being better with it than I am."

"No, sir," Tracy answered truthfully.

" 'Cause you're always welcome to try, boy, you're always welcome to try."

"Thank you, Mr. Ethan."

Ethan laughed. "Christ, you still got something uppity about you, ain't you! Well, I'll tell you, I think we just gon' match you in a real fight soon. How'd you like that?"

"No, thank you."

"Sorry, you ain't got no choice. . . ."

One morning as he was about to go to the fields to join his work gang, he came across Alexandria waiting for him behind Ethan's barn. Almost three weeks had passed since she had left him, and he hadn't so much as seen her during that time.

She greeted him with an uncertain smile, and he felt an unexpected pang. "I wanted to be sure you're all right," she said.

"I'm all right. How's he treating you?"

She shrugged. "Like this, like that. You know."

"I only know that he frightened you. You once said he was the kind of man who lived only to hurt people."

"Don't worry. I'll be all right." She laughed, but her laughter had pain in it.

Tracy looked at the girl, realizing for the first time how much he had missed her. He had missed her face, her presence, the husky Creole music of her voice. And he wanted to tell her, *Listen, we're leaving here. Help is on its way, or will be soon.* But he didn't dare. He dared not take the slightest chance that Ethan might find out.

Instead he said, "Alexandria, don't give up. We're both going to get away from here yet."

She shook her head. "There's no way out, Sugar. I
175

made myself face that. Oh, maybe there is for you—you can run for it—"

"If I ever do, I'll come back for you. I promise."

"You just take care of yourself. Now, let's not get caught together. . . ."

Each evening after dark he made a discreet entrance into the mansion, where Hannah awaited him. The door was always unlocked, and she was always alone. They had a drink or two, usually in her office, and they talked of old times, or he told her stories of his life on the river, or they sat in brooding silence.

They remained acutely aware of each other as man and woman, and with increasing discomfort. He was afraid to be alone with her for very long. After a half-hour or an hour, he would stand up to signal his departure.

"So soon?"

"Hannah, I'm a tired man. And I have to rise early and toil in your fields."

"I tried to get you out of them."

"I know—don't worry about me."

"My ole Tracy. . . ."

Each evening she would kiss his cheek—he made it difficult for her to do more—and he would hurry away. On Sunday evening, she was unreasonably angry with him for not having come to her earlier in the day.

"Why, you could have spent the whole afternoon here if you'd wanted to!"

"Yes, and had deep trouble. It's dangerous enough, just visiting you evenings—"

"Oh, don't try to fool me! You probably got yourself a new wench by now—"

"Hannah."

"Or maybe you arranged to meet that Alexandria of yours somewhere—"

"Hannah."

"Christ, you men, you're all alike. All you think of is your cocks—"

"*Mrs. Hannah!*"

"I'm sorry, Tracy. I'm just plain ole female jealous is all. You know, in a way, you're all I got. Got no man in my life. Know plenty women, but I don't like them, and they don't like me. Miz Barclay, she hates my guts. So you're about all, and soon I'm gon' lose you."

She tried to insinuate herself into his arms, but somehow he managed to evade her.

The next three evenings went easily, as if Hannah had determined to keep distance between them. After a half-hour, she made it plain that she was ready for him to leave, and he did so. But on Thursday evening he had a third drink, and it was all too easy to stay. An hour slipped by and then another, and then he didn't care when he left. He slipped lower in his comfortable chair in the office and realized that Hannah was getting drunk.

She talked. "You probably can't understand why I married him. I can't either. But he was there. Always expected to. Didn't seem to be anybody else to marry. So . . .

"Lost two babies first six months we were married. That's not so much, is it? Lots women lose two, three babies for every one they get to keep. But the doctor, he says maybe I can't have no more. Ethan, he got real mad about that. He spent a whole year trying to knock me up, and I mean that's about all he *did* do that year, morning, noon, and night. . . ."

She sprawled in her usual chair, by the desk, a single lamp burning low and yellow nearby. From time to time, she lifted her face into the light and paused, breathing hard to burn the liquor she had never learned to handle, and then her head would fall forward, her black hair shadowing her face.

"If you think I enjoyed that, you don't know nothing about Ethan. Before long, he made pretty clear I weren't nothing to him but a dang brood bitch. He wanted to whelp a son out of me, because then, all I had would surely be his. No doubt about it. His son, my heir. I don't think he even much *liked* servicing me 'cept when he hurt me. He *liked* hurting me . . .

"When it really got bad was after my ole daddy died. Before then, he had to be careful, but afterwards . . . I found out about the other women pretty quick—their friends all started hating me like it was my fault what Ethan was doing. But that wasn't the worse. We was living up at the other place then, you know, Ethan's. He was spreading me less and less, and I had an idea he was into the slave wenches. One day I came back from town and found him and two of the wenches stark naked. In my bed. I came back down here to my place, and I been here ever since . . . Oh, Jesus, Tracy, I'm gon' be sick!"

He hurried her out to the kitchen and helped her to empty her stomach, then he made her drink deeply of cold water.

"Can you get to bed?"

"Help me. Help me up the stairs."

They went staggering up the long stairs, she directed him along a hallway, and they entered a dark bedroom.

"Now, you get plenty of sleep and you'll be all right."

"Put me to bed."

He opened the mosquito bar with one hand, then lifted Hannah in his arms and lowered her onto the bed. She pulled his head down to hers, and when she kissed him, he didn't resist. Warmth flooded him. *Just this once,* he thought, and he returned the kiss, his arms around her.

"Oh, thank God," she moaned. "Kiss me again."

This time her tongue fluttered over his, and for an instant, the darkness seemed to be filled with flashing lights. The shock of desire was exquisite as it took command of his flesh.

"Been wanting to kiss you properly," Hannah whispered, and as their mouths met again, she brought one of his hands to a hardened nipple.

He had to stop, he knew he should leave, but his mouth, his hands, his body had their own will. He continued to hold her in the dark, to kiss her, to stroke her. She tried to draw his hand down her body, and somehow he managed to pull the hand away. She touched him instead, and again the lights flashed.

"Tracy," she whispered, "you want to pleasure me?"

One great effort: "I'd better go—"

"No, wait." She brought both arms tightly around his neck for an instant. "Do you remember the last time I saw you before Aunt Rachel and me went to England? How I said I'd never forget the things we done together?"

"Yes."

"I never forgot those things. Did you?"

"Never, Hannah."

"And I said I'd remember how we went swimming and kissed and loved each other."

"I remember."

Her whisper was hot against his ear in the darkness. "And remember how I teased you 'cause you was excited?"

"Hannah—"

"I pretended I didn't care, I even pretended to myself. But I *did* care. I was trying to make you want me, because I wanted *you*, Tracy, I wanted you, and I still do want you—"

He tore himself away from her.

"God damn you!" she sobbed.

"You know this is no good," he panted. "You know—"

"I know it's five years since I even been *touched!* And how much longer you think it's been since I took pleasure in it? I know I want you and you want me! And, for Christ sake, if my aunt was good enough for Simon, why ain't I good enough for you?"

"You're drunk, that's all. You're drunk, and it wouldn't be right."

"And if I was sober?"

He didn't answer. He was already hurrying from the room.

The great temptation was to turn around immediately and go back. He had been without Alexandria for weeks, and he needed a woman. Hannah had aroused him, and she wanted him. She was there for the taking.

And furthermore, he still loved her in some way, whether he wanted to or not. She was the same Hannah he had known as a child, the same Hannah he had played with and kissed and loved when he was a boy. The same Hannah who had taken seven lashes of a field whip for him. *Yes, damn it,* he thought, *she's still mine!*

The next morning he tried to avoid thinking of her. Instead, he concentrated on the hard work of clearing drainage ditches, and when he thought of anything else, he thought of a letter, an answer, from Fayette. He had to *know* that she was taking steps to obtain his freedom; mere hope was a kind of torture.

When evening came, Hannah reentered his mind and refused to leave it. He thought she was probably expecting him in the big house despite the humiliation of the evening before, but he determined to stay away. Wanting each other as they did, his visiting the mansion was too danger-ous. If she had any news from Fayette, she would surely bring it to him.

The following day was grim. He couldn't maintain, or even fake, the high spirits he had been displaying, and three times the whip fell on his shoulders. Once he nearly turned on his driver, and he managed to restrain himself only at the last possible instant. Fortunately it was a Satur-day, and the work gangs left the fields early.

He washed up and went to the cookhouse for his sup-per. He was tempted to go see Hannah, but he resisted. Instead, he spent an hour in the slave quarters, listening to the music and watching the dancing. Then, despondent, he walked back to the cottage.

She was waiting for him, sitting in the darkness like a white shadow. His door had a lock, but he had never both-ered with it; there was nothing left in Simon's cottage that anyone would want to steal.

Neither of them said a word while he lit a lamp. Then he turned to her and saw that she was holding a letter. And her face told him that all hope was gone.

" ' . . . so good to hear from you," Tracy read, " 'and you cannot imagine how pleased I am to know that Tracy is alive and well. He chose a life with many dangers, and it is long since I last heard from him, but I have thought of him often.

" 'Yes, I remember his stay with me in Ohio well. We are in this world to serve, and I only wish I could have served him more wisely. I have no idea what your father may have told you of the views I held, dear cousin, or what Tracy has told you of our relationship, but I must confess that I was led dangerously astray in many respects. And with God's aid, I have, as it were, repented and recanted. I no longer hold the utopian views that were mine for so many years, and I recognize the fact that abolitionism is the devil's doctrine, a challenge to the God-given right to hold slaves.

" 'Please do not misunderstand. I have not forgone *all* of my former views. I still believe that the *practice* of slavery is all too often fraught with evils, which must be eradicated. Lynching, branding, lack of adequate physical and medical care for slaves—all this is enough to make a Christian woman weep. If we are to exercise the God-given right to hold slaves, we must do so responsibly. We are responsible for these poor half-human creatures' bodies and whatever souls they may have, and we must never forget this.

" 'In short, along with the right goes an obligation. And further, as long as there are blacks among us, we are obliged to *hold* them as slaves. Slaves need masters, and a free black is a danger to the purity and sovereignty of the white race. When free—male and female alike—they appeal to the lowest instincts of the white man or woman, tearing us down to their level, and making animals of us all.

" 'You will understand, then, how happy I am to know that Tracy is back where he belongs. I think of him with great fondness, and I am sure he will be well cared for under your benevolent ownership. And you will understand that I cannot in all conscience vouch for the fact of his freedom. Indeed, had I any such manumission document as you refer to in my care, I should be obliged to burn it . . .' "

"Poor Fayette," Tracy said.

"Poor Fayette!" Hannah's voice shook with anger. "Do you realize what that woman is doing to you?"

Tracy nodded.

"May she burn in hell," Hannah raged, "may the bitch burn in hell. Tracy, I've been sick at the thought of losing you, but I never wished you this. Not once did I wish you this—"

"I'd like it if you left me alone."

"There must be something we can do—"

"There's nothing. Please leave me alone."

Avoiding Hannah's eyes, he went into the dark bedroom. He didn't bother to undress, simply pulled the mosquito bar aside and threw himself down on the bed. He felt as sick and defeated as he had ever felt before in his life. He had put absolute faith in Fayette, because that was his last hope. And now faith and hope had been destroyed.

The light in the other room went out, and he heard Hannah leave.

He lay where he was, scarcely moving, for more than two hours. The sounds of the slave quarters died down, and night settled in.

He sat up and listened to the stillness of the night for a few minutes. Then he left the bed and felt his way through the darkness to the door of the cottage. He opened the door and went outside as quietly as possible.

He stood still for a moment, breathing the night air, scarcely cooler than the day. The stars and the moon were brilliant. In the slave quarters, a single, stringed instrument twanged lonesomely.

There was always a watchman, and Tracy, waiting in the shadows, watched him appear and then vanish again around the corner of the barn. He hadn't seen Tracy, or if he had, he had ignored him. Tracy walked quickly but unhurriedly across the yard to the back door of the big house. There were no lights showing behind the windows. The back door was, as usual, unlocked, and Tracy entered the dark house.

He called Hannah's name softly. There was no answer.

Still in the dark, he made his way to the office, calling Hannah's name several times. As he had expected, the office was deserted. He left it and went up the stairs to the next floor. Steps creaked beneath his weight.

He had been to her bedroom only once before, but he had no difficulty in finding it. The doorway was wide open, and he stepped into the room.

"Hannah."

He heard her startled gasp behind the mosquito bar as he crossed the room toward the bed.

"Who is it? Who's there?"

"Don't be frightened. It's me—Tracy."

She yanked the netting aside, and moonlight struck her bare body.

"Tracy . . . oh, God . . . are you really here?"

"I'm here." He began unfastening his shirt.

"Are you—are you going to? . . . Oh, God . . . oh, my God . . ."

She lit a lamp on a table beside the bed. By the time she had it aglow, he had his clothes off. She held out her arms as he went to her; her head went back as he leaned over her, and she kissed him hungrily.

"Hurry," she whispered, and he climbed into the bed with her. "Now. Don't wait."

When he took her and she cried out, "Oh, I love you, I love you, I love you," he answered, truthfully enough, "And I love you." But it was not love that he felt.

It was despair.

PART FOUR

chapter one

The barn was bright with torch light and the flickering red light of smudges that supposedly drove away the mosquitoes. Ethan Flynn and half a dozen other white men were present, together with a dozen slaves, including several wenches. Tracy recognized one of the Colby brothers and the man named Follett, but they showed no sign of recognizing him and no special interest in him. Perhaps they knew better than to do so.

Tracy looked at the white circle, a dozen feet in diameter, painted on the floor of the barn, and a wave of nausea went through him. This time it was no mere training session. It was not a game except to the white masters who stood around the circle watching. This time the steel in Tracy's right hand carried an edge.

His sickness grew as on command, he stepped into the circle; his opponent, a young man called Cicero, didn't look as if he felt much better. Cicero was lean and wiry, with exceptionally long arms, and his very black chest, shoulders, and forearms were laced with long pink scars. He had been handsome once, but now his face carried several ugly gashes.

Cicero used a fencer's stance and began a swift little dance as he and Tracy stepped toward each other, and Tracy felt a touch of confidence he had lacked before. The twelve-foot circle gave them little room, put the bout at close quarters. Tracy didn't mind this in the slightest, as he had developed a watch-and-wait style, but Cicero obviously felt constricted.

Cicero danced from side to side, his point creating slithery serpentines in the air. Tracy tracked him from a standstill position, barely pivoting, and keeping a steady point. A flashing knife no longer dazzled him, and he no longer tried to follow its patterns; he merely watched for his opponent's true attacking movements and his failures of defense.

He saw Cicero hesitate for the merest fraction of a second. Then Cicero lunged forward, his right arm straight out, his blade going for Tracy's face. A flash of panic; Tracy swung up his right forearm to fend off the thrust, but he struck air. Cicero had dropped low, and his knife was cutting upward from Tracy's waist to his right nipple.

There was an instant of shock, of numbness. Then Tracy felt the sting of the cut, and the blood rushed out. In the next instant sickness and fear gave way to anger, and he wanted to slash back without mercy; but his arms were seized, and he was dragged out of the circle. Cicero backed warily away.

One of the drivers who had helped train Tracy examined the wound and pronounced it a mere scratch. Still, it was first blood for Cicero. Tracy, trembling now, was returned to the ring.

Why was he fighting this man whom he didn't even know?

He was fighting because a small group of gamblers had grown bored with cards and were looking for something more exciting. Because Ethan had bet a thousand dollars on him against two thousand on the more experienced Cicero. Because he would be brutally punished if he refused to fight. And because of Alexandria.

"We got to give these boys something to fight for besides just getting out of a whipping," Ethan had said.

"Ain't that right, Tracy? What you think we ought to give you and Cicero here to fight for?"

Tracy had said nothing.

"No suggestions? Well, I think I got something you boys might like." Then, after calling Alexandria into the barn, he had grinned at Tracy. "You won her once, boy. Thought you might like to try again. Or maybe you'd just as soon let Cicero have her?"

Now Alexandria was standing to one side, trying to maintain the indifferent air she had had on the first night Tracy had seen her, trying to hide sickness and shame and fear, and he felt that he had betrayed her in the first heat through a failure of nerve. It would not happen again.

Cicero was an aggressive fighter, but this time he was slower to mount his attack. Tracy *felt* that his opponent didn't know how to handle the constriction of the twelve-foot circle. He also remembered the slight hesitation before the feint to the face. He was beginning to know what to watch for with this man.

Cicero began to move, to dance, and the onlookers fell silent. The only sound was the quick shuffling, skipping sound of feet. As before, Tracy hardly moved, merely keeping a straight point, he wanted to encourage Cicero to use again an attack that had already succeeded once.

And in the end, he did exactly that. Tracy was well guarded except for the face, so after that brief telltale hesitation—Cicero lunged for the face. But this time, Tracy made no attempt to parry his attacker's arm. At the very instant of the attack, he counterattacked, throwing himself forward and past Cicero. As he fell, he whipped the knife over the man's belly and heard him gasp. Then he hit the ground, rolled, and came to his feet, point forward and steady, as if they had been fighting one heat for a kill.

He had been well trained.

This time Cicero was taken from the ring. Fortunately, his wound, too, was superficial; the kind of attack Tracy had used could very easily have taken his guts out.

The third heat was over almost before it had begun. Tracy took direct advantage of Cicero's feeling of constriction. The moment they were both within the white line, he walked quickly and directly toward his opponent, to all appearances hardly maintaining his guard. He was careful not to rush and cause Cicero to lash out wildly, and he didn't so much as glance at Cicero's knife. In fact, until the very last instant, he didn't even look at Cicero.

With all his experience, Cicero was caught off guard. He didn't know what to do, and there was no place to which he could retreat to decide. He tried to keep Tracy away by slicing air, and Tracy had his gambler's feeling of having constructed a successful bluff. He caught the man's wrist easily, stepped in, and flicked his blade lightly across Cicero's chest. Cicero caught *his* wrist, but by then it was too late. Third blood was Tracy's.

He had to win only one more time.

He looked at Alexandria. She had her hands over her face, and her shoulders were bent. She swayed, and he had a feeling she was close to fainting.

Ethan laughed and patted Tracy's shoulder and told him how clever he was.

The fourth heat was the long one. Suddenly, inexplicably, Cicero seemed to adapt himself to the twelve-foot circle. His dance steps and his knife movements were more subtle, slower, more snakelike. He advanced on Tracy slower than before yet more aggressively, and he seemed intent upon dominating no less with the eye than with the knife. Tracy found himself backing away, following the edge of the circle.

To his alarm, he found he couldn't stop his retreat. Cicero was mounting no major attacks now. Each one was merely tentative and hardly signaled by the hesitation Tracy had observed earlier. None gave him the slightest opportunity to counterattack, and within a few minutes, his right forearm had half a dozen small cuts. None served to end the heat—only a body cut would do that—but his arm began to tremble badly.

He could think of only one thing to do. He tried to swing to the middle of the circle in order to put Cicero's back to the line. It was a mistake. He had no idea what went wrong, but suddenly Cicero's knife was slicing him across the chest from his left shoulder to his left armpit. The sensation was like ice followed by fire, and a purely animal cry escaped from his throat. He fell backwards to the floor for fear Cicero would strike again, and he stared at the blood welling up out of his chest. He was dragged out of the circle.

One of the drivers wiped the blood away, but it continued to flow. Tracy wasn't sure he could go on, though he knew he had to for Alexandria. For the first time, he realized that he was sweating as well as bleeding, and the sweat stung his wounds.

"Once more," Ethan said. "You can take him."

"How?"

"Easy. Just never repeat a mistake."

"Mr. Ethan, I'm cut up. I'm bleeding bad, worse than him—"

"Oh, for Christ sake," Ethan sneered, "men been hurt worse in fist fights! You got any guts, nigger, either you're gon' spill them in that circle, or you're gon' spill his out!"

No, there was no choice. He had to go back, he had to finish it. This time he went to the center of the circle before Cicero could start backing him up, and he stayed there. The other man danced slowly around him, making little forays, but Tracy refused to do anything other than pivot and keep a straight point.

After a moment, Cicero spoke for the first time, his voice a harsh whisper. "You gon' get yourself killed, boy."

"If I have to," Tracy answered.

"Now, why you want to do that?"

"To cut you down."

Cicero's eyes widened. He understood. "Hey, now," he said soothingly, "this just a friendly little—"

It was the mistake Tracy had been waiting for, watching for, hoping for. Actually, he had made it himself in answering Cicero. One of the first things he had learned was never to talk while fighting at close quarters, and when your opponent spoke—strike then. For an instant, his reaction time would be drastically cut down. So when Cicero, startled, worried, spoke for the third time, Tracy grabbed his right wrist.

"No!" Cicero tried to grab Tracy's right wrist, knowing

the attempt was futile, knowing what was going to happen.

Tracy evaded the clutching hand and brought his knife ripping up, and Cicero screamed.

And it was over.

They gave him whiskey, and he immediately vomited. Then Alexandria led him from the barn, his shirt thrown over his shoulders and a bundle of rags clutched to his chest to stay the bleeding.

Mosquitoes whined about him, they scenting blood, but he hardly noticed. His teeth chattered and his knees shook. The night darkened as if the stars were going out, but he knew the darkness was really in his head: he was close to fainting. He staggered, and Alexandria tightened her grip on his arm.

"Just a little farther, sugar . . . just a little farther . . . and soon you'll be home. . . ."

Then suddenly his head cleared. He felt weak, and his legs were unsteady, but the worst of his shock was over. The stars were back in their places, and the night was crystal clear. A few hundred yards away he saw light from the Carter slave quarters.

He stopped and took a deep breath, releasing it with a long shuddering sigh.

"It's all right now," he said.

Alexandria looked uncertain. "You sure?"

"Yes. You can go on back."

"Not yet. I been looking for a chance to talk to you."

He didn't want to talk; he wanted only to be with Hannah. "Let's wait till another time—"

"It's got to be now," Alexandria said urgently. "We mightn't get another chance for a month, and you could get yourself killed before then."

"That's the truth." Tracy laughed weakly. "All right, talk."

"It's about you and that woman, you got to leave her alone—"

"Me and what woman," he asked, startled, "what are you talking about?"

"Sugar, you know damn well what woman, your own

192

sweet Miz Hannah is what woman, and she's gon' get you killed yet. Can't you stay away from her, for God's sake?"

For a moment he could only stare at Alexandria, all his illusions of safety dispelled. He and Hannah had known the risks, but they had been so careful. Now it seemed to him that the surrounding darkness must be filled with unseen eyes and ears, and he instinctively lowered his voice.

"There's nothing between Hannah and me."

Alexandria stared back at him, obviously doubtful. "You swear to God?"

"I swear to nothing. Where did you get such a damn fool idea?"

"I heard it. I met two or three people here I can believe, and they say you been shagging that woman regular for weeks. You mean it ain't true?"

"If it was, do you think I'd be crazy enough to let anyone find out?"

She shook her head impatiently. "Honeychile, true or not, that kind of talk can kill you. And I got a bad feeling about Mr. Ethan lately—he's got something on his mind."

"You think he suspects something?"

Alexandria considered for a moment, then shook her head. "No. If he did, you'd be dead already. But if you're smart, you won't get near that woman, and I'll do everything I can to stop the talk about you and her."

"Thank you." Tracy reached out and touched the girl's cheek, and she immediately took his hand.

"You were fighting for me tonight, weren't you," she said, "so I wouldn't have to do nothing with that Cicero."

"Well, I did make you a promise."

She shook her head. "You were free from that when I left you. But I do thank you. . . . You want me to go on with you and fix up your cuts?"

"No, they're not as bad as they look. You better go on back."

"All right. I'm gon' keep an eye on that Mr. Ethan. I tell you, I've got a bad feeling. . . ." Alexandria looked back the way they had come. She seemed reluctant to leave. "Well . . . you won me once, and you won me twice . . . and if you ever want anything from me . . . I'll be there. . . ."

He watched for a moment while she disappeared into the night-shadows, then he went on toward the Carter mansion.

Though it was late, there were still sounds from the slave quarters, and lights burned steadily and beckoningly in a couple of mansion windows. Tracy looked carefully about the yard and, seeing no one about, slipped quietly in through the back door.

Hannah was waiting for him in the kitchen, and when she saw him, she uttered a little scream.

"It's all right," he said quickly, "I'm all right."

"But my God, look at you!"

For the first time since Alexandria had led him out of the barn he did look at himself. The rags that he clutched to his chest were soaked with blood, and so were his hands, his ragged pants, even his boot tops. He hadn't realized he had lost so much blood.

"Just a few scratches on my arm and chest and one real cut," he said. "Long as they don't fester and turn feverish I'll be all right."

"Goddam Ethan used you in a knife fight, didn't he!"

"He won two thousand dollars on me."

He was surprised to hear a touch of pride in his voice, but Hannah told him precisely what Ethan could do with his two thousand dollars.

She pulled his shirt from his shoulders and had him step out of his blood-soaked pants and shoes while she fetched a basket of clean white rags that had been saved specifically for bandaging. Next, as Tracy leaned back against the pump sink, she very carefully drew the wet rags from his chest. Part of the slanting cut had ceased to bleed, but it started again as she bathed his chest with whiskey. The liquor hurt far more than the slice of the knife had.

"Do you have to do that?" he asked, gasping with pain.

"You know Simon always said whiskey was best."

Jaw set and eyes hard as stone, Hannah worked quickly and efficiently: this was far from being the first wound she had dressed. She knew exactly how to draw the strips of cloth over the cut to discourage further bleeding and to minimize any scar. Within a few minutes, Tracy had a jacket of bandages over his ribs and shoulders, and the blood was no longer coming through. She then cleansed and bandaged his right forearm.

"Now I got to wash you up," she said, looking with disgust at his blood-sticky body.

"I can do it."

"Don't be crazy. You move around much, you'll soon be bleeding again. You want a drink of whiskey first?"

"I think I need one."

She poured a stiff drink for each of them, and this time his stayed down. Then Hannah went back to work, jaw still set and eyes still hard. Using water cold from the pump and harsh yellow soap, she washed him virtually from head to foot, splashing water and suds in every direction, yet carefully keeping the bandages dry. When every trace of blood was gone, she briskly toweled him, never pausing for an instant until she was done.

At that instant, the hardness abruptly left her eyes, and her jaw went slack. The towel dropped from her hands, but her hands continued to move over him. With a sigh, she threw herself against him, and he found himself needing her, perhaps more urgently than ever before. He had just fought a dangerous contest and survived. And now he was with his woman. His arms locked her to him, and his mouth opened over hers.

"*Goddam!*" As abruptly as she had embraced him, Hannah tore herself away, turning and hiding her face. "What the hell is *wrong* with me! I can't keep my hands off you anymore! Here you are, all cut and bleeding, and me acting like a bitch in heat!"

"You come back here."

"I'm sorry, Tracy—"

"Don't be."

He pulled her back into his arms and set his mouth to hers again.

"Do you really want to?" she asked when he allowed her to speak.

"I'm going to, if not with you, then another. Now, are you my Hannah or not?"

"You black bastard," she groaned, "I love you, and you know I'm yours. . . ."

She led him, not up the narrow back staircase, but through the front of the house so that they could remain in each other's arms as they went. In the great front hall, she drew her dress over her head and flung it away, and he thought of the day eleven years before when she had done the same thing in a sun-sparkling stream. Still embracing, they climbed the stairs and followed the hallway to her bedroom. Beside the bed a lamp gave out a steady yellow light.

"You see," she said, "I been waiting for you, and the way was already lit. But you've been hurt, so now you got to do exactly what I say. . . ."

He did do as she told him, lying back on the bed, and soon her hair sheltered him from the light. It fell like a dark curtain on each side of his face as she knelt over him and bent forward to kiss him.

"Now I got you," she whispered. "You're mine."

"Yes."

"And I'm yours. Nobody else's."

For long minutes, they remained still in their embrace, never speaking.

And then, "Tracy."

"Yes."

"I know you love your freedom more than you love me—"

"Sh. Don't talk."

"I got to say this. You turned hell into heaven for me. I want to do the same for you. And this is the only way I know how. This is the only thing I got to offer you."

"Right now," he said, "this is the only thing I care about."

"I'm so glad. We ain't never gon' let nobody take this away from us, are we?"

"Never."

"You're all I got, all I got, all I got. . . ."

Her whispers died away, and for a time, what they had was enough. She cried out first and then he, and their cries subsided into the soft laughter of relief.

"Oh, I love you," Hannah said happily, "and I ain't never gon' lose you, never, never, never."

"Very touching," Ethan Flynn said, "but I'm afraid you're wrong."

Ethan lounged with lazy ease against the frame of the doorway, and the knife in his hand caught the light of the lamp. It appeared to be the same five thin inches of carbon steel he had carried eleven years before. He was grinning as amiably as if he had just played an innocent practical joke, but Tracy knew that smile, and if froze him. Hannah had thrown herself off of Tracy the instant she had heard Ethan's voice, and now she looked at her husband, not with the slightest trace of fear, but with utter contempt and loathing.

" 'You turned hell into heaven for me,' " Ethan said mockingly, " 'and I want to do the same for you.' "

"You been standing there all the time, standing there watching and listening."

"Not all the time, woman, but long enough."

Hannah sat up on the bed and leaned toward Ethan. Her voice, when she spoke, was as venomous as any Tracy had ever heard.

"More than once I called you filth, Ethan, but I never knew what filth you are. What walking, crawling filth. And I'll tell you what I hope for you, Ethan, I hope you die. I hope you sicken and die and do it soon. Die fast or slow, I don't care, I just want to dump you into a pit and get you out of the way. So go away and die, Ethan, and then I'll pray to Christ you go to hell forever."

Ethan's smile twitched, and he thumbed the blade of his knife. "Somebody's gon' die all right," he said, "but it ain't gon' be me."

He left the doorway and walked toward the foot of the bed, staggering slightly, and Tracy saw that his drinks were telling. He tried to estimate his chances of jumping and overcoming Ethan, and decided they were almost nonexistent. A man who had just lost a pint or more of blood and then taken his woman was not in the best possible condition to fight for his life.

Ethan looked down at Hannah, his face rich with revulsion, but still smiling, always smiling. "Jesus, look at you," he said, "bareass naked and stinking of nigger and just don't give a damn. All these years you been telling me you don't do no nigger-fucking, and here you are. Been doing it since you was maybe thirteen, fourteen years old, I guess—"

"You shut your filthy mouth!"

"I sure called it, didn't I? Said you liked nothing better than a black boy hot from the battle. To be honest, woman, I never really thought I'd catch you. But then I guess I'm just lucky." He glanced at Tracy. "When that Alexandria wench came back so soon, I had a feeling I'd better look after you, boy."

Hannah seemed to be caught in a paroxysm of hatred. Her entire body shook. "I hope you die, I want you to die, damn you—"

"Shut up and tell me what to do with you, woman," Ethan said softly. "Tell me what you think we ought to do?"

Hannah's eyes widened and fear began to show in them.

"All of a sudden, got nothing to say," Ethan went on. "Well, I'll tell you. I suppose I could get away with killing you right along with this here black boy. Or I could get me some witnesses up here and then get me a divorce and leave you with nothing. But then I'd be rid of you, and hell, I don't want to be rid of you. No, ma'am, and you're never gon' be rid of me. 'Cause I'm gon' make you pay for being what you are. You understand me?"

Hannah didn't answer, but her eyes now showed that she understood. And Tracy understood that, no matter what the odds against him, he was going to have to try to kill this man.

"Yes, you understand," Ethan said. "So I'll tell you what we're gon' do. We're gon' finish what ought to been done when I caught you with this here nigger boy eleven years ago. We're gon' call all the niggers from both these plantations together. And we're gon' invite every white man, woman, and child for miles around. And then we're gon' show them that any white woman 'round here that acts like a nigger gets treated like one."

"You ain't gon' whip me—"

"Not me, I don't have to whip niggers. I got Barclay for that."

"You wouldn't dare—"

"Woman, don't say I wouldn't dare. I can come and go from Louisiana as I please, and what people around here may think of what I do, I just purely don't give a damn. Barclay's gon' give you a hundred rawhide lashes, and that's just for openers. Before I'm done with you, no man, black or white, is gon' want you in his bed, not ever again. And when you can't take that no more, you can go hang yourself."

For the first time since Ethan had entered the room, Hannah attempted to cover herself, pulling the bed spread up in front of her body. Ethan swung his attention to Tracy, gazing down at him and whetting his knife with his thumb.

"Why ain't you running, boy?" he asked.

He took a step toward Tracy, and Tracy stood up from the bed and backed away. And at that very instant, Alexandria appeared behind Ethan in the doorway, a cocked revolver clutched in both hands.

"If I was you, I'd start running right now," Ethan said, taking another step. "I wouldn't stop to put on no pants nor shoes nor anything else. 'Cause we gon' be after you soon, and the sooner you start running, the longer you got to live."

Alexandria came silently through the doorway and raised the gun, aiming it unsteadily at Ethan's back. Her eyes were wide; she was obviously terrified. Tracy realized what had happened. Keeping watch on Ethan, she had followed him here. She had heard voices and understood the situation, and she had taken the gun from Hannah's desk. Tracy struggled to keep his eyes on Ethan and away from Alexandria.

"And it won't be like the last time," Ethan continued, "not like eleven years ago. We'll have our sport with you, and we'll catch you. But this time when we put you on your back and I put this knife to you—"

"*Kill him, kill him, kill him!*" Hannah screamed.

Ethan stiffened as if something cold had touched the

small of his back. The gun shook visibly in Alexandria's hands.

"Kill him, kill him, kill him!" Hannah screamed.

Alexandria stood paralyzed.

Ethan turned quickly but without apparent haste and looked at Alexandria. With one hand he sheathed his knife while he pushed the muzzle of the gun aside with the other, and then he took the gun from Alexandria's hands. He laughed quietly to himself and shook his head. He lowered the hammer on the weapon. Then with all his strength he threw it through a window, and it fell into darkness in a shower of broken glass.

Ethan looked at Tracy one more time. "Run, nigger," he said, and he left the room.

For several seconds no one moved. Then Alexandria ran to Tracy and threw herself into his arms. She was shaking, and he held her tightly. Hannah rushed from the bed to a wardrobe and pulled out a dress.

"I'm sorry," Alexandria said after a moment.

"It's all right."

"It's not all right! Tracy, you've got to run!"

"There's no place to run to."

"Oh, my God, and if only I'd killed him . . . But I just couldn't do it. I said if you ever wanted anything from me, it was yours, and then I couldn't kill him. I had the gun in my hands, it was loaded and cocked, and yet I couldn't pull the trigger. *Why* couldn't I kill him, Tracy?"

"Maybe because you've been told all your life that you couldn't hurt a white man—we're just slaves. Maybe I couldn't kill him either." He thought of the gun lying on the ground somewhere below. "But by God, I'm going to try."

Noticing for the first time that Hannah was gone, he put Alexandria out of his arms. She followed him as he hurried from the room and down the back stairs to the kitchen. His bloody clothes still lay there, strewn about the floor, but he had no time for them now. He had to find the gun. He took the lamp from the table and hurried out into the back yard.

"There!"

It was Alexandria's startled cry. Hannah was ahead of

them. Ethan was disappearing into the darkness on his way back to the Flynn plantation, and Hannah, gun in hand, was running after him.

Tracy followed with only one thought in mind: to get that revolver for himself.

He reached Hannah just as she caught up with Ethan. Ethan had heard her coming and turned around. When he saw the gun, he smiled, the same lazy grin that had played over his handsome face most of his life.

"Woman, what you think you doing?" he asked.

"Ethan," Hannah said quite distinctly, "I am going to kill you."

He held out his hand. "Give me that gun."

"Go to hell."

He wrapped his fingers around her wrist.

She pulled the trigger, and the flash lit up his face as the bullet drove into his chest. He was still smiling, but his eyes held a look of ineffable surprise. His face disappeared as he fell over in the darkness.

Then they watched him die.

chapter two

At the sugar house a dozen voices disturbed the evening with wild cries of triumph, and the cries quickly spread through the darkness to the slave quarters. Someone rang a cowbell, some others banged on iron pans, and an old cavalry trumpet blared joyously. "All right, goddammit," Tracy shouted, "you all can break out them jugs of whiskey now and take out your fiddles! 'Cause we done it! We done it!"

He walked wearily away from the revelers, happy for them that they still had the energy to celebrate. Autumn brought the heaviest work of the year on a sugar plantation, and the last weeks had been exhausting.

He locked the door behind him as he entered Hannah's house, and in the kitchen, he turned up the lamp. With disgust, he discovered that she had no hot water waiting for him. Goddam woman. Well, he would have to wash with cold. He stripped off his clothes, primed the pump, and began working the handle. Fresh clothes were waiting for him in a cabinet, and after he had washed and changed, he felt better.

Hannah, as he had expected, was in her office working

on her books. She barely glanced at him as he entered the room. She was wearing a neat and clean blue dress—neither the black of mourning nor her usual tattered cotton. He had noticed that she was paying more attention to her appearance each day, and this was just one of the changes that had gradually come over her since her husband's "unfortunate accident." She went into town more frequently and eagerly, and she talked increasingly about the people she met there. She visited neighbors as she hadn't in years. She was clearly astonished to find that there were many people who wanted to know and to like her. Few had shed tears over Ethan's death.

"What was that commotion out there?" she asked, still poring over her records.

Tracy sank into a chair. "Celebration. Last hogshead filled and everything cleaned up. I told them to break out their liquor and their fiddles."

Now Hannah at last looked at him, and she frowned, puzzled. "What the hell are you talking about?"

"Just what I said. Not a drop of juice left to boil."

"But that's impossible, Tracy. It's still more'n two weeks till Christmas. We never finished up that early before long as I can remember."

"You did this year, lady."

Hannah laughed. "Hey, now, that's wonderful! You want us to celebrate, too? Wait a minute, I'll get us something to drink."

While she went after the liquor, Tracy closed his eyes, relaxed in his chair, and wondered, *How am I going to tell her?* She returned in a few minutes with a bottle of French brandy and two glasses. She poured the liquor and passed a glass to Tracy. They sipped, and Tracy tried to find the right words.

"Guess you'll be heading upriver right after the New Year," he said.

Hannah nodded. "The new overseer seems to be working out, and I think I should look over the other plantations as soon as possible. The sooner they find out I'm the boss and mean business, the better it will be. Don't you think so, Tracy?"

"I agree."

"I'll need your help, of course. I figure we can leave the first week in January—"

"Not we, Hannah. You."

Her eyes widened. She knew what was coming, she had known for weeks, but she tried to put it off.

"You don't want to come with me? You want to stay here?"

He shook his head. "You know what I want."

"No. No, I don't. What do you want that you don't have here? What could you possibly want?"

"My freedom. Mine and Alexandria's."

Hannah gulped her drink. Her hand shook as she poured another. "Sometimes I think you're in love with that fancy bitch," she said.

"You know better."

"I don't know nothing!" Hannah said angrily. "I don't know . . . I don't . . ." Anger collapsed into tears, and she walked the room with her hands over her face. "Oh, Tracy, what the hell's wrong with you? You got everything here—"

"Everything but my freedom."

"I thought you loved me!"

"I do—"

"Then *how* can you just go off and leave me?"

"Because we're natural enemies."

She turned on him. "Now, that just don't make sense! You're the best friend I had in my whole life, and I always been a friend to you. We fought for each other and took whippings for each other and loved each other. How can you look at me and say we're natural enemies?"

"You hold slaves."

Hannah straightened as if he had slapped her, and for a moment, her eyes went blank.

"Well, of course I hold slaves," she said weakly.

"Are you ready to let them go free?"

"You know I can't do that. I reckon I *could* turn a profit without them, but the thing is, I'm responsible for them—"

"Like your cousin Fayette."

"No, not like her at all! Now, don't you twist my words! I'm responsible because how'd they take care of themselves? They ain't all like you and me, Tracy. They don't know how to take care—"

"You could teach them."

Hannah slowly shook her head. Her tears had stopped, and she looked bewildered. "Tracy, I can't change the way the world works—"

"Neither can I. But I can do something about my small share of it. And that's why I've got to leave here—so I can take care of my share."

"But you can have a share right here!"

"No, I can't. Simon felt he had to stay here to care for his, but I've got to go."

Hannah grasped at a straw. "Simon and my Aunt Rachel, they were happy—"

"Simon was miserable, and he went crazy and nearly killed you. The important thing is that I forgot a lot of things he taught me. I forgot what freedom and slavery were all about. I thought I had my own little world separate and apart from the big black-and-white world, a world of my own where I could hardly be touched. But I was wrong, wasn't I? I know now that I was. And do you understand now why I say we're natural enemies?"

She turned quickly away from him without answering. He went to her and took her shoulders.

"Hannah," he said gently, "I was willing to stay with you 'til we were sure there'd be no trouble about Ethan's death. I was willing to help you run the place until you were rid of Barclay and had a new overseer. But you've known all along I'd be leaving soon. We've talked about it. And now I want to be free."

"You're free right here," she said, her voice muffled.

"No, I am not."

"You're free right here with me, and you got no damn right to call me your enemy."

"I'm sorry."

She turned in his arms and embraced him, burying her face against his shoulder, and again she wept. And he knew that however much she might protest his leaving, she would let him go.

"When do you figure to leave?" she asked when at last her tears had subsided.

"A day or two. As soon as you'll let me."

"Do you really think we'll ever see each other again?"

"I'll let you know where I am from time to time, and if you really want to see me . . ." He remembered how he and Fayette had drifted apart.

"We could travel north together in January. That's only a few weeks off.

"The longer we wait, the harder it's going to be, Hannah. For me, too." He rocked her in his arms and kissed the top of her head.

She sighed. "And who will hold me like this and listen to my bad dreams and pleasure me after you're gone?" she asked.

"You're a rich woman, and you're going to be traveling a lot, meeting a lot of people. You're going to have all the men you want in your life."

"Don't want none in my life but you."

She lifted her head from his shoulder. She looked into his eyes as if she were trying to read something in them, trying to see something special, and for a moment, he felt that he could never bear to leave this woman.

"Tracy," she said, "you are a fool. You know the love we got between us, and you're willing to throw it away. Well, I ain't. I lost you once eleven years ago, and now I am going to lose you again. I know I can't keep your love by holding you here, so I'm letting you go. But I'm coming after you, and I'm gon' get you. Want to bet on it?"

"You're on," Tracy said.

Tracy Carter stood at the rail of the *Duchess of Cairo*, heading north from New Orleans, and listened to the hoot and boom of the riverboats in the night and watched the passing lights on boats and the shore. Down the Mississippi River the boats came, down the "Main Street of America," and then back up again they went. Up to Baton Rouge and Natchez and Vicksburg, up to Greenville and Memphis and Cairo, Illinois, and then further north to St. Louis and beyond, or eastward, following the Ohio River to Paducah and Louisville and Cincinnati. Tracy suddenly realized he loved the boats and the rivers. He loved the whole damned country in an odd sort of way. Too bad it didn't much love him.

He left the rail and went to the gambling lounge. He had been pleasantly surprised to find his job waiting for him. Not that it had been kept open for him, but he was needed. His whole system of operation had begun to break down soon after he had disappeared, and no one had been able to save it. Now he was being asked to put it back into shape again.

My kingdom, he thought as he walked among the green tables and the glittering lights, *my own little world.*

But it wasn't simply his own little world any longer; it was part of the big world. And that was a lot of world to put back into shape. He wondered how much of it was really his fair share.

"I tell you this, boy, and my curse on you if you ever forget it. As long as any one man in this world is a slave, no man is free. He may not know it, he may not want it, he may be afraid to admit it—but no man is free! And that is not just some kind of Bible talk, Tracy—that is the Godawful truth they use to help keep us trapped!"

He had forgotten once. He would never forget again.

BEST SELLING PAPERBACKS FROM CORONET INCLUDE

DAVID NIVEN
☐ 15817 4 The Moon's A Balloon   40p

ROBIN MOORE
☐ 15089 0 The French Connection   35p

CHARLES M. SCHULZ
☐ 10595 X Here's To You, Charlie Brown   20p

KURT VONNEGUT Jr.
☐ 02876 9 The Sirens of Titan   30p

MARTHA ROFHEART
☐ 16530 8 Cry God For Harry   50p

NIGEL TRANTER
☐ 17836 1 Lord and Master   45p

R. F. DELDERFIELD
☐ 02787 8 Farewell The Tranquil Mind   35p

MILTON SHULMAN
☐ 13176 1 Defeat in The West   50p

P. R. REID
☐ 02406 2 The Colditz Story   30p
☐ 01180 7 The Latter Days at Colditz   35p

ERICH SEGAL
☐ 12508 X Love Story   25p

All these books are available at your bookshop or newsagent, or can be ordered direct from the publisher. Just tick the titles you want and fill in the form below.

CORONET BOOKS, P.O. Box 11, Falmouth, Cornwall.

Please send cheque or postal order. No currency, and allow the following for postage and packing:
1 book – 10p, 2 books – 15p, 3 books – 20p, 4–5 books – 25p, 6–9 books – 4p per copy, 10–15 books – 2½p per copy, over 30 books free within the U.K.
Overseas – please allow 10p for the first book and 5p per copy for each additional book.

Name...

Address ....

....